STAR WARS™

ATTACK OF THE CLONES

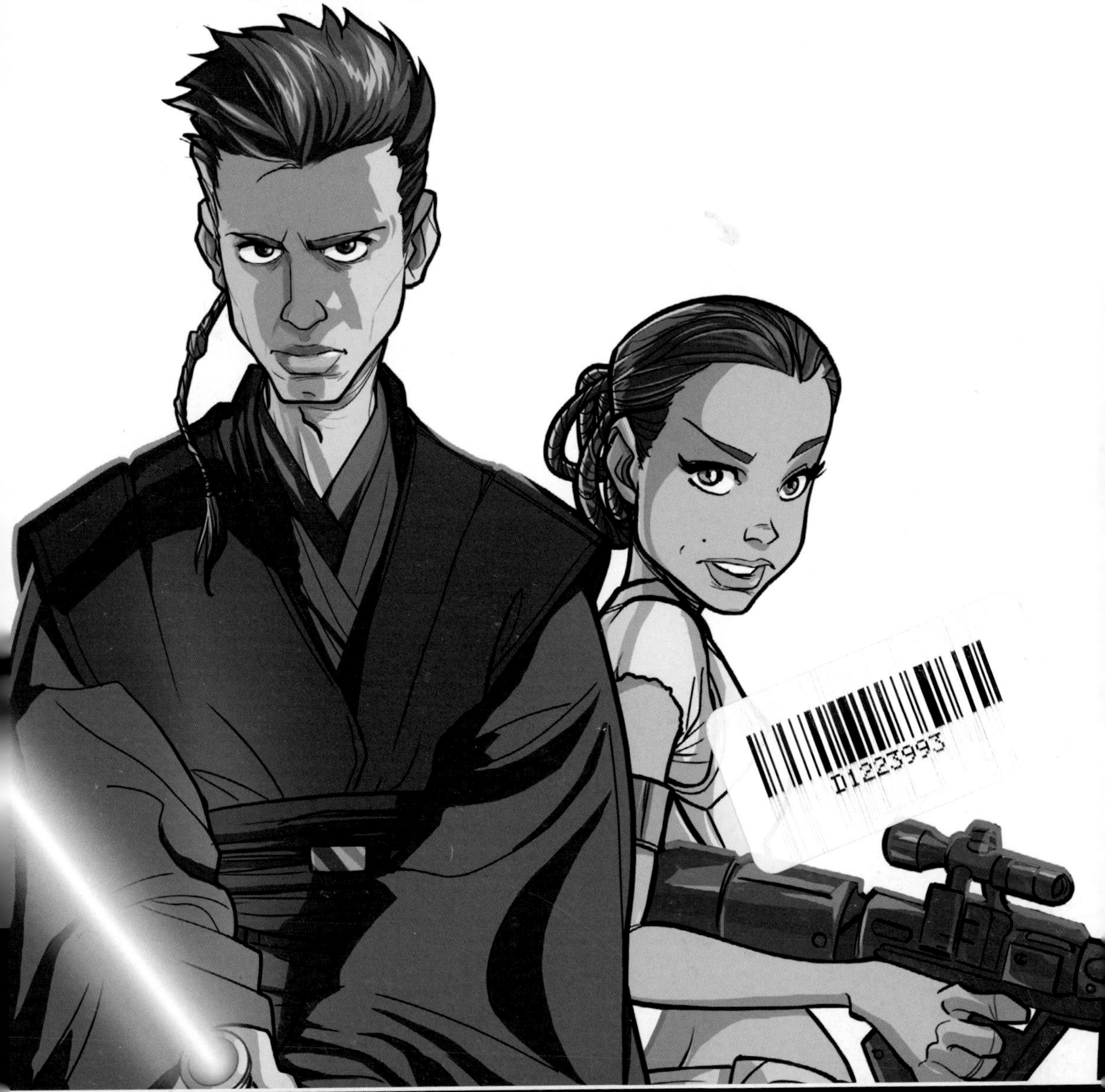

A LONG TIME AGO IN A GALAXY FAR, FAR AWAY....

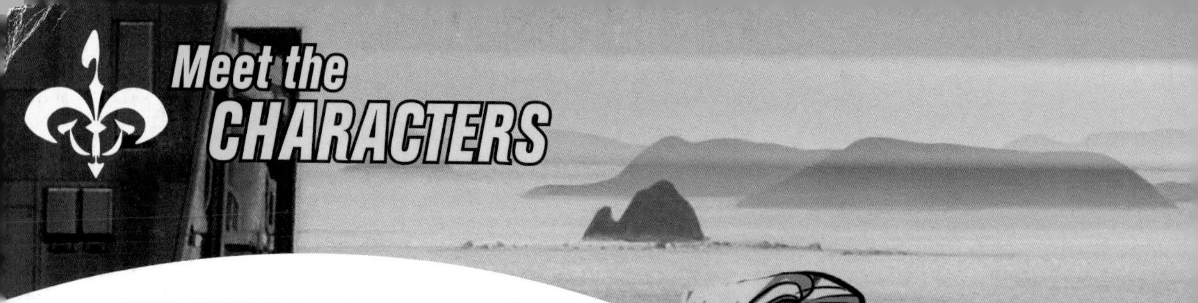

Meet the CHARACTERS

SENATOR AMIDALA

Now a member of the **Galactic Senate**, **Padmé Amidala** continues to protect her home planet with devotion and dedication. For security reasons, she travels disguised as a Naboo pilot when she returns to the Galactic capital of **Coruscant**.

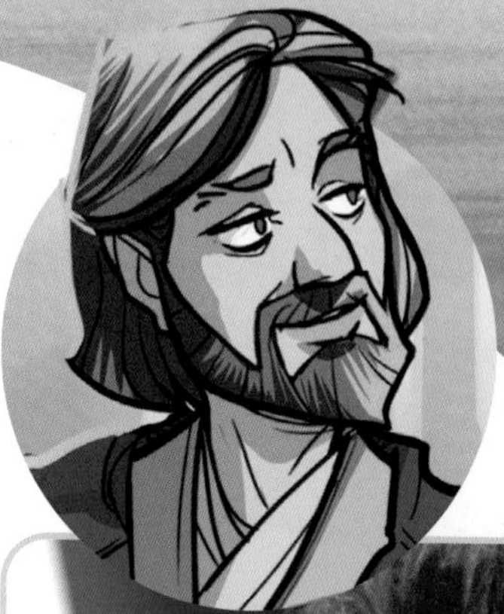

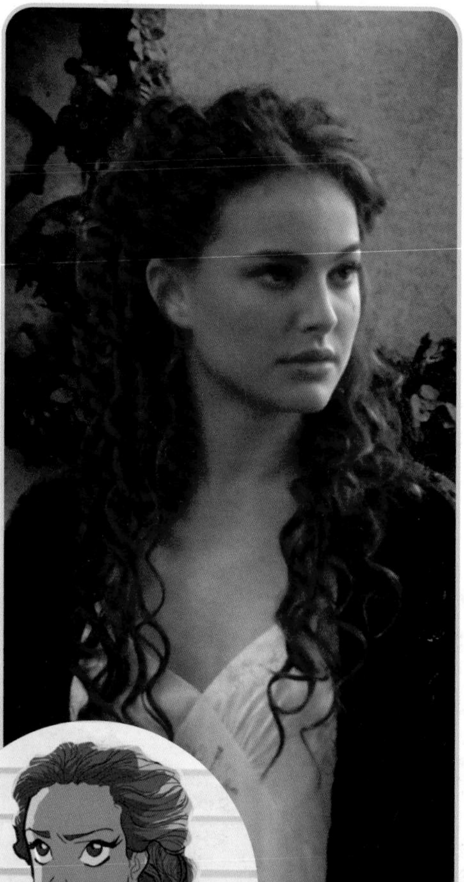

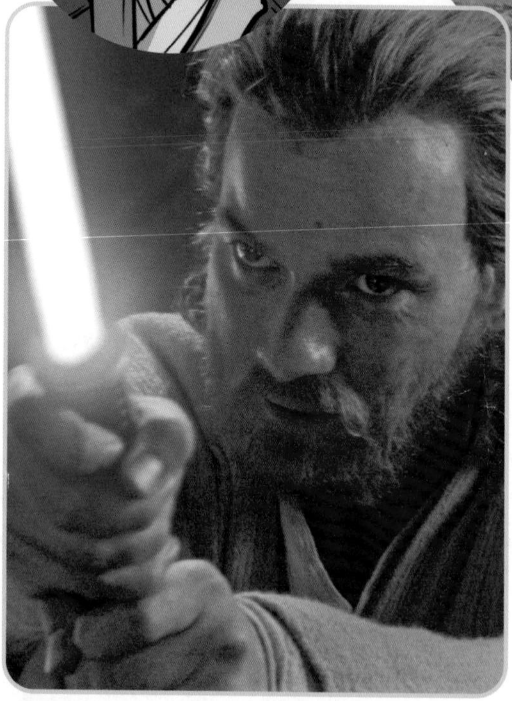

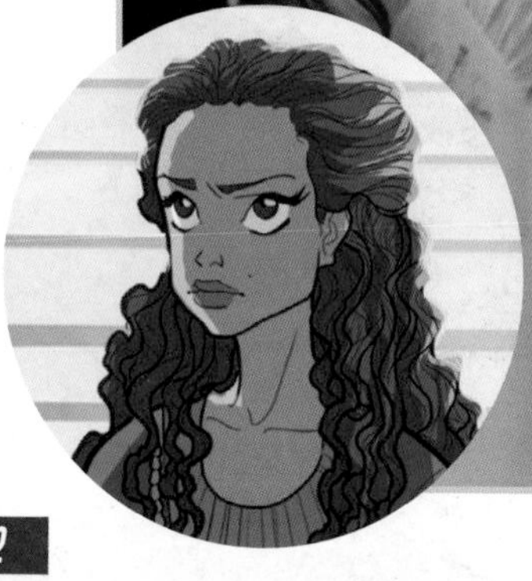

OBI-WAN KENOBI

Fulfilling the promise made to his former master, **Qui-Gon Jinn**, Kenobi took Anakin Skywalker as his **Padawan** and is now training him in the ways of the Force. A cautious and thoughtful mentor, Obi-Wan is also a skilled **swordsman** and a **brilliant strategist**, but he always goes for diplomacy first.

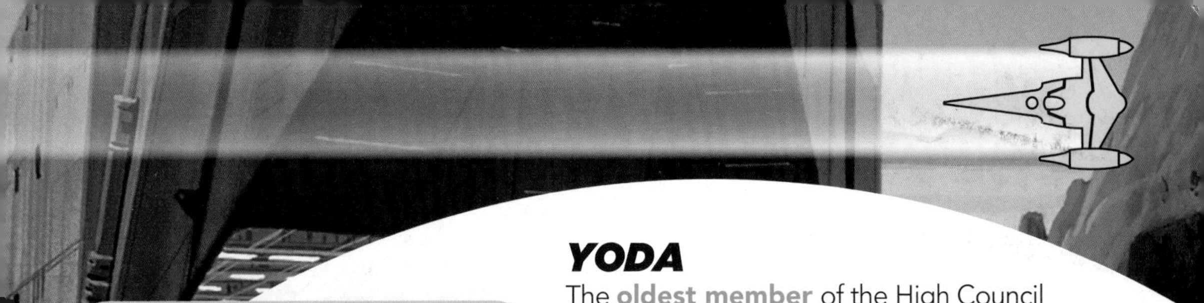

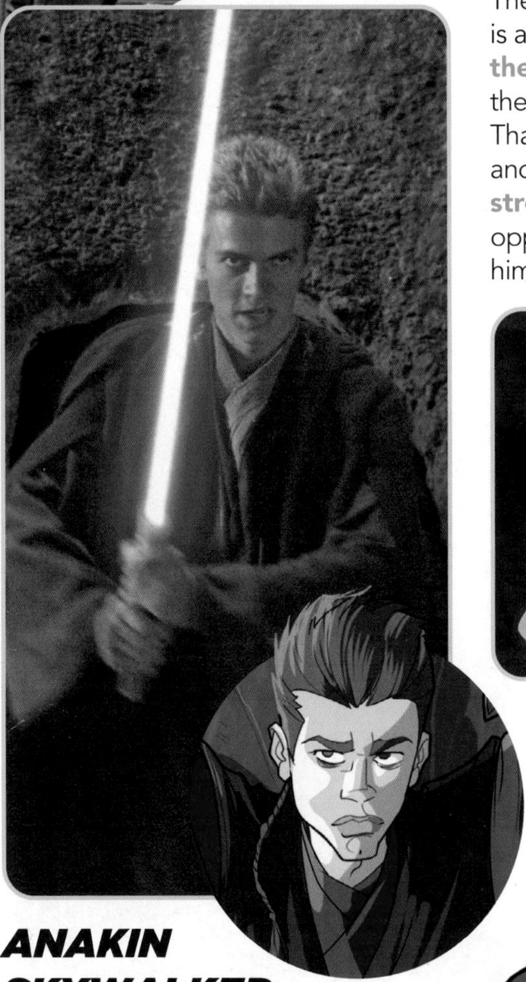

YODA

The **oldest member** of the High Council is also one of the **most powerful Jedi in the Galaxy** and the only one who can feel the threat of war looming over the Republic. Thanks to his strong bond with the Force, and his training, Yoda has amazing **strength** and **speed**. And no opponent can hope to overcome him in lightsaber combat.

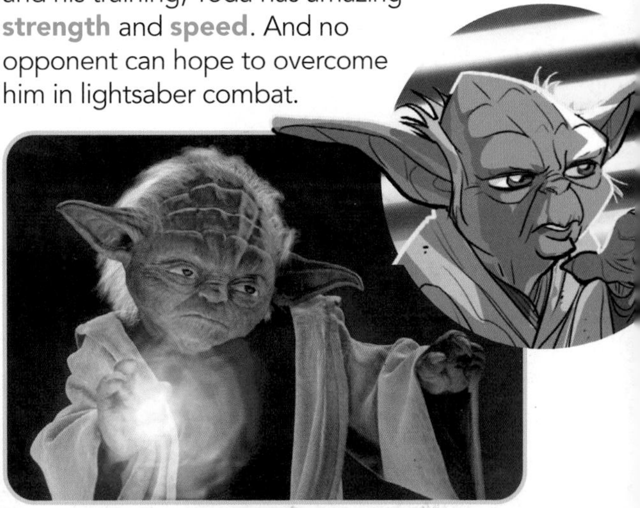

MACE WINDU

Mace Windu is a **senior member** of the Jedi High Council. His **wisdom** and **swordsmanship** are legendary, as is his devotion to the Order and to its duty: to **serve the Republic** and to **protect peace at any cost**.

ANAKIN SKYWALKER

Gifted with unusual **Force skills**, young Anakin is already one of the **best pilots** and **fighters** in the Jedi Order. But he is also too **impatient** and **impulsive**, unwilling to follow his Master's orders most of the time. As Yoda and the **Jedi High Council** members suspect, moreover, Skywalker cannot resist feelings of **love** and **hate**.

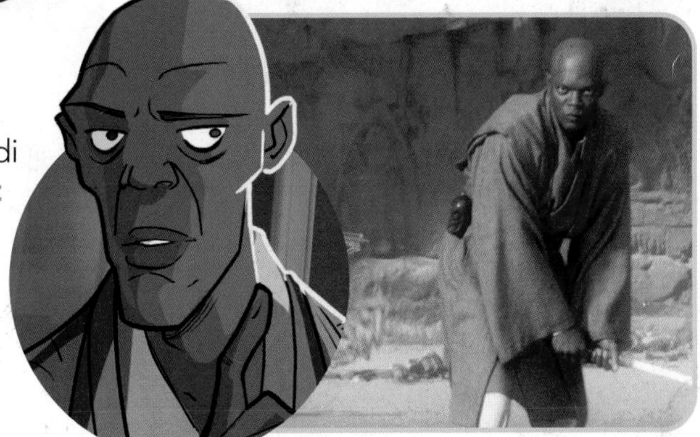

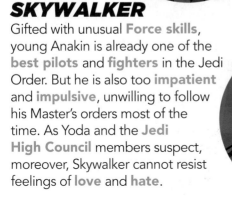

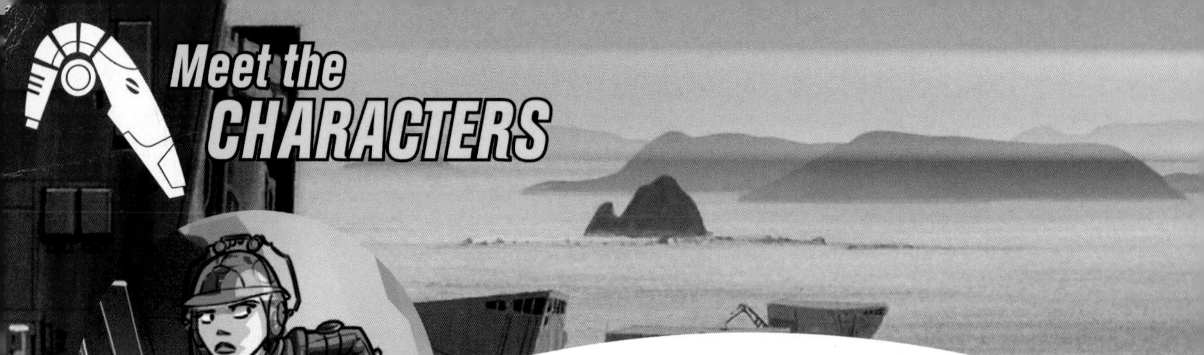

Meet the CHARACTERS

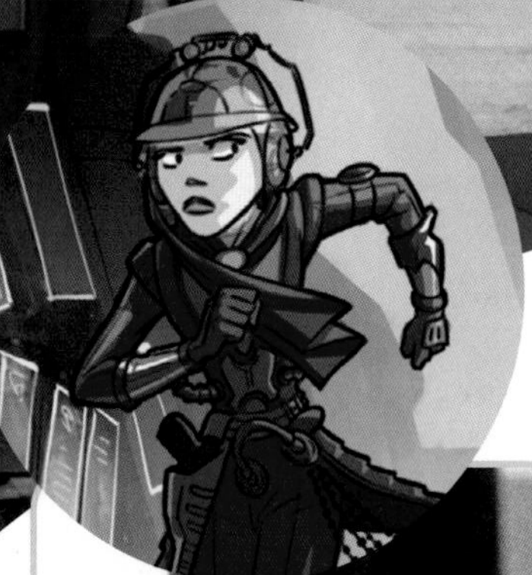

JANGO FETT

Outfitted in **Mandalorian armor**, Jango Fett is an extremely skilled **bounty hunter** for hire. His armor is equipped with many armaments, including a **jetpack**, a **dart shooter**, an **explosive missile**, **blasters**, and a **whipcord thrower**.

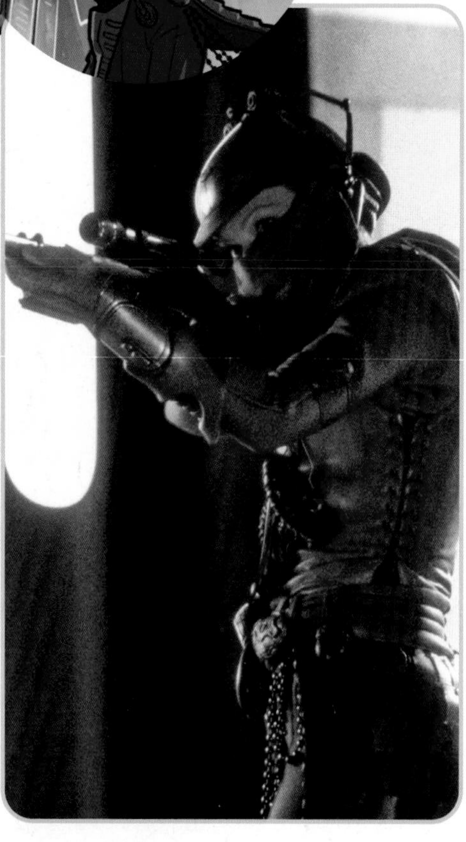

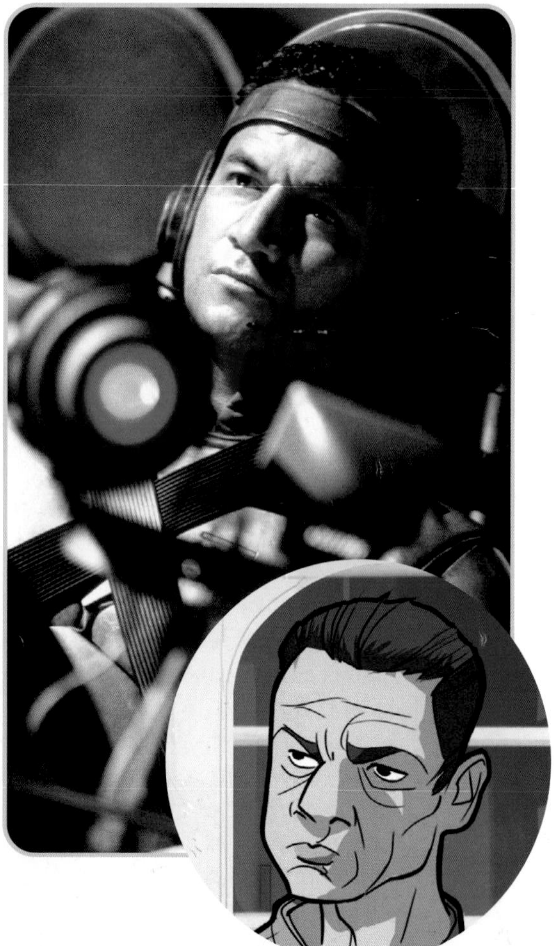

ZAM WESELL

A professional killer and a talented bounty hunter, Zam is a **shape-shifter** and can change her appearance to mimic any humanoid being. When she is hired to kill a target she usually employs **kouhuns**, small arthropods with a lethal **nerve toxin**.

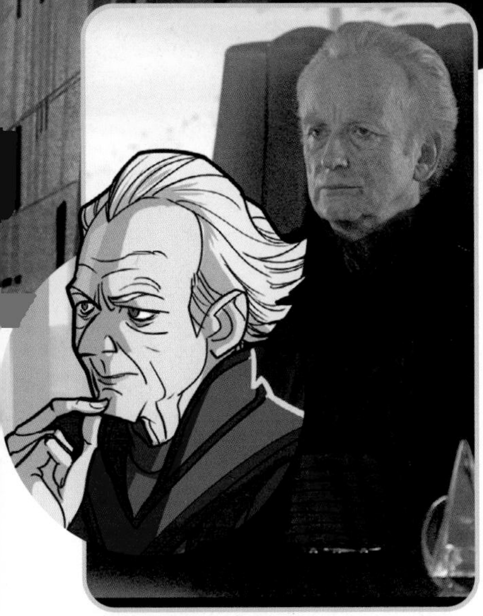

COUNT DOOKU

Once a **Jedi Master**, Dooku secretly joined the dark side, becoming **Darth Tyranus**, Sith apprentice to **Darth Sidious**. Since then, his powers have **increased enormously**, and he is now able to even cast the powerful **Sith lightning**. Dooku is an elegant and outstanding swordsman and a natural leader.

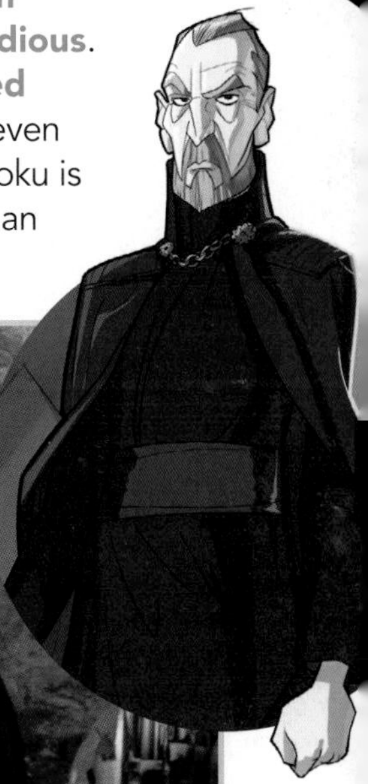

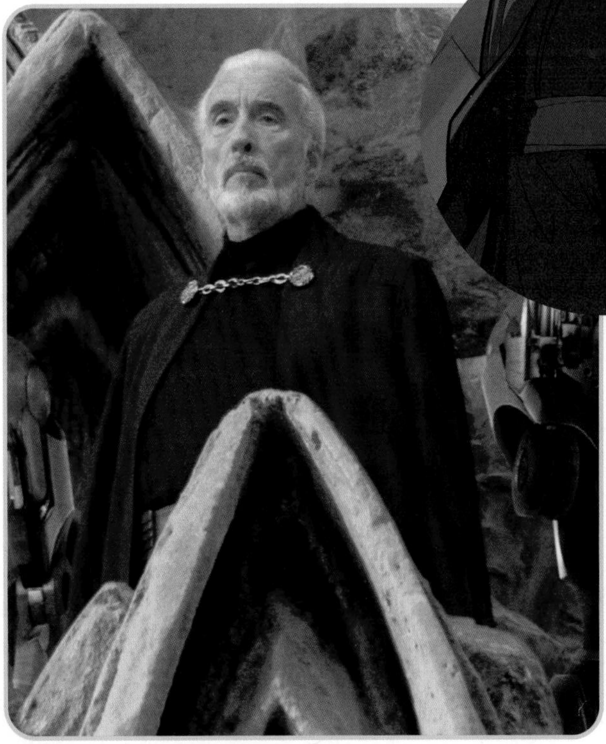

SUPREME CHANCELLOR PALPATINE

His **relentless rise to power** made him Supreme Chancellor of the **Galactic Senate** ten years ago, but the rise may not be over: the **new crisis** demands a strong leader, and Palpatine claims to be ready to play that role.

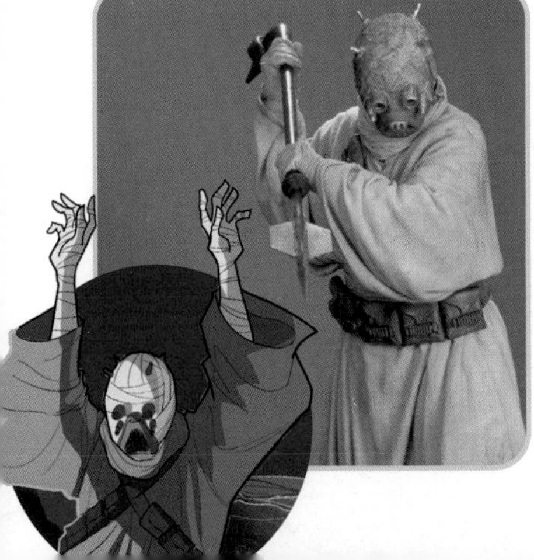

TUSKEN RAIDERS

Primitive and violent people indigenous to Tatooine, Tusken Raiders live in the **Jundland Wastes** and slay anyone who comes near their wells, for they believe water is sacred and promised to them only. Divided by clan, the **Sand People** (as they are also known) often attack travelers and moisture farmers – their most hated enemies.

Episode II
ATTACK OF THE CLONES

There is unrest in the Galactic Senate. Several thousand solar systems have declared their intentions to leave the Republic.

This separatist movement, under the leadership of the mysterious Count Dooku, has made it difficult for the limited number of Jedi Knights to maintain peace and order in the galaxy.

Senator Amidala, the former Queen of Naboo, is returning to the Galactic Senate to vote on the critical issue of creating an ARMY OF THE REPUBLIC to assist the overwhelmed Jedi....

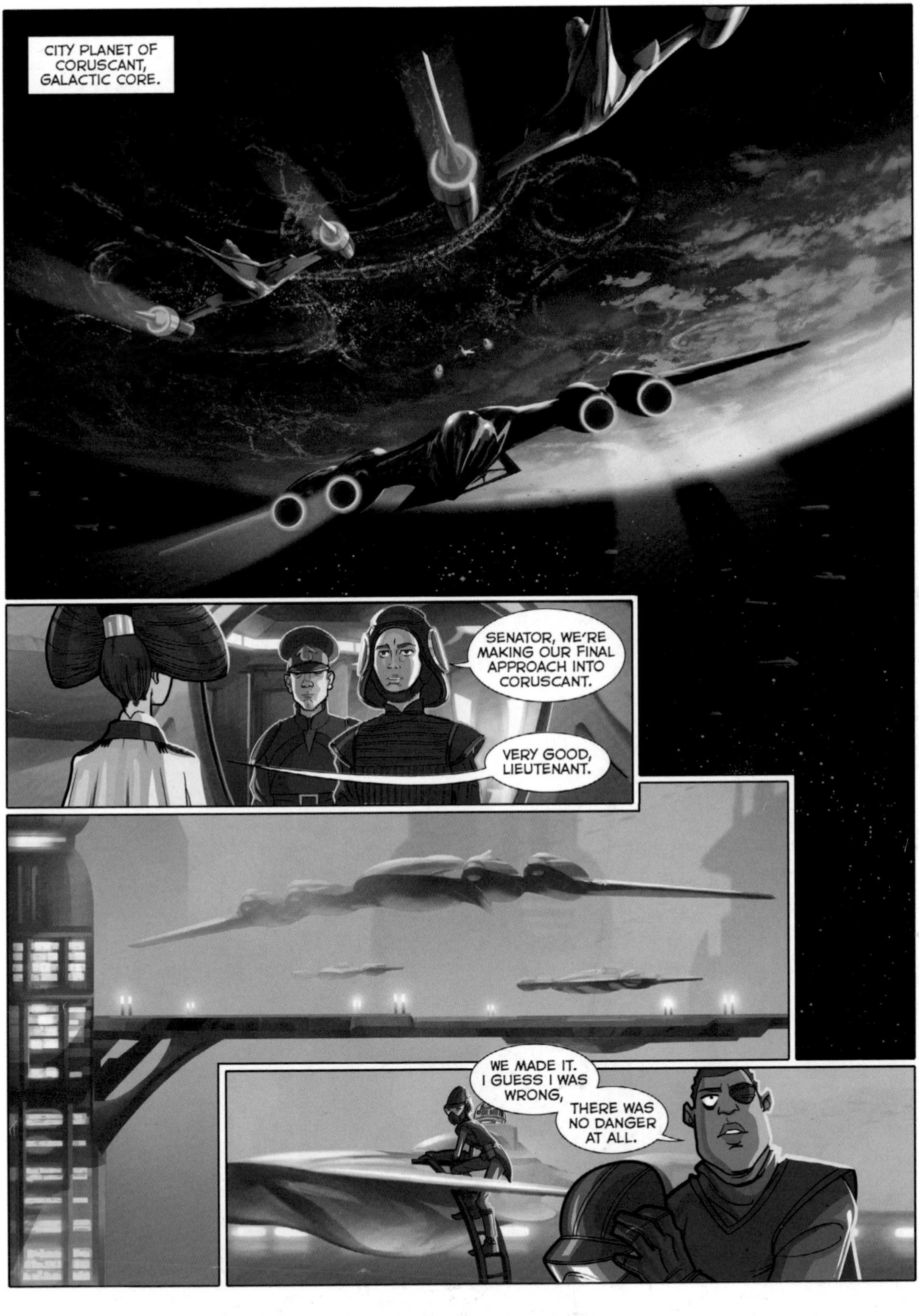

CITY PLANET OF CORUSCANT, GALACTIC CORE.
SENATOR, WE'RE MAKING OUR FINAL APPROACH INTO CORUSCANT.
VERY GOOD, LIEUTENANT.
WE MADE IT. I GUESS I WAS WRONG,
THERE WAS NO DANGER AT ALL.

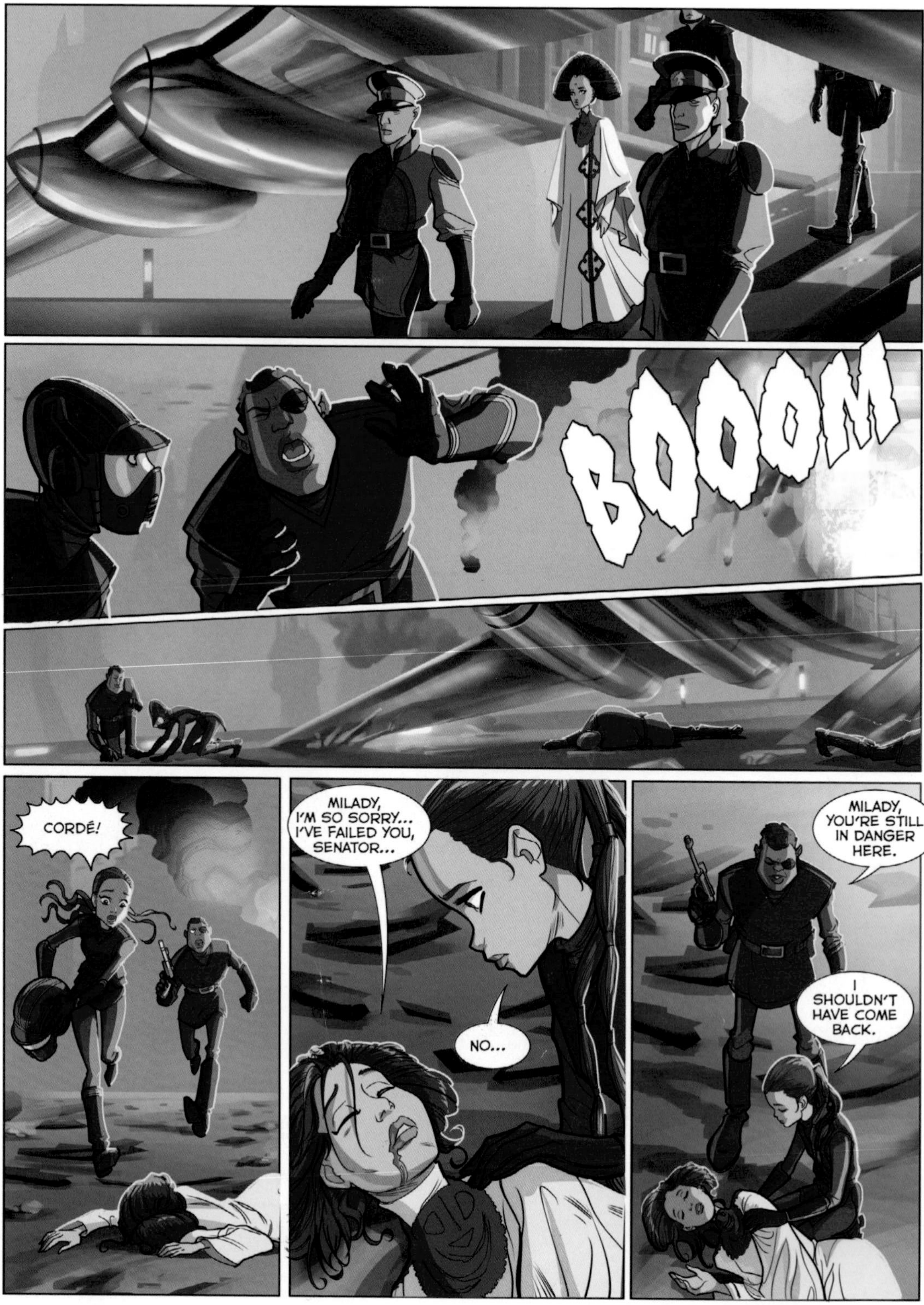
BOOOM
CORDÉ!
MILADY, I'M SO SORRY... I'VE FAILED YOU, SENATOR...
NO...
MILADY, YOU'RE STILL IN DANGER HERE.
I SHOULDN'T HAVE COME BACK.

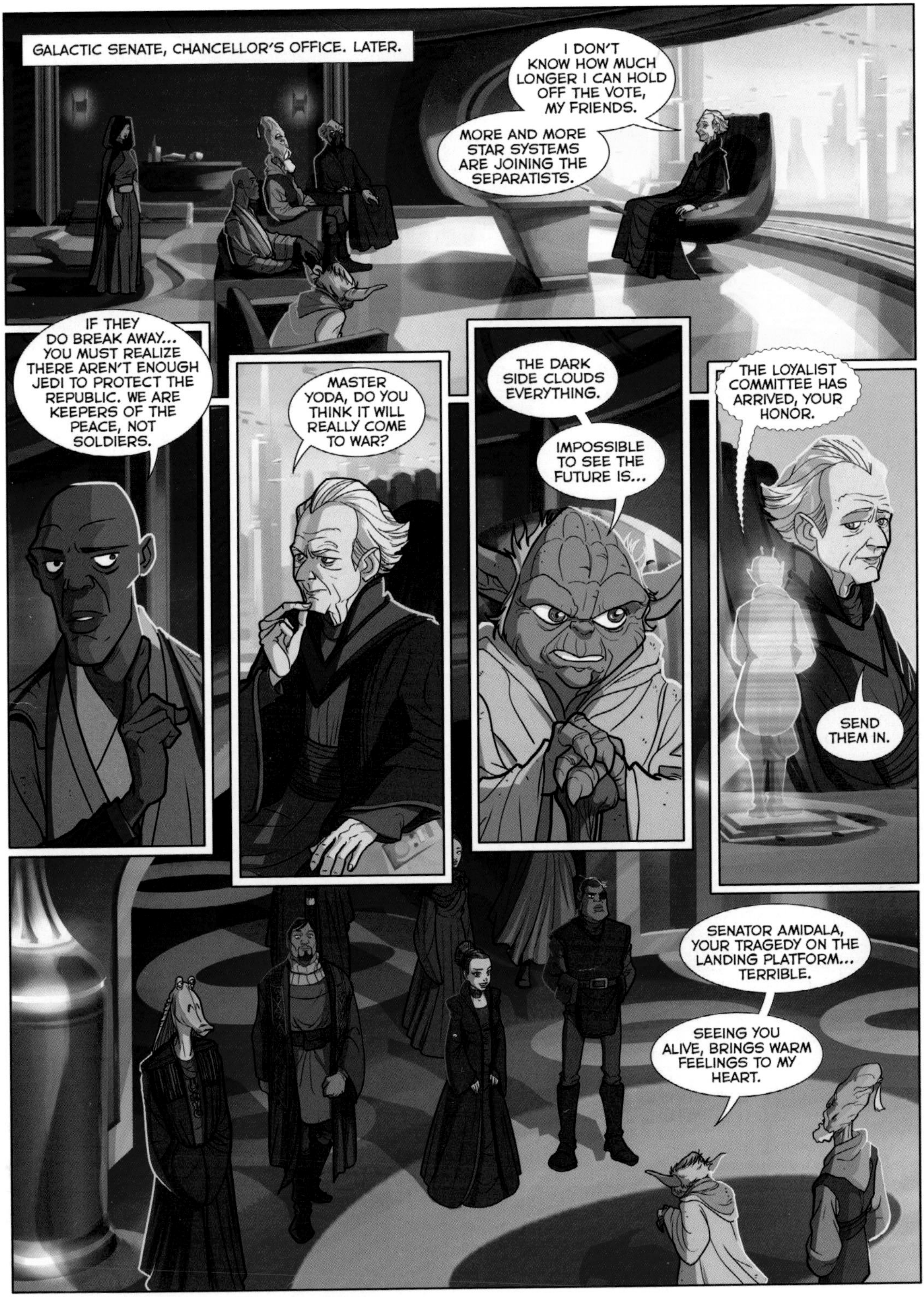
GALACTIC SENATE, CHANCELLOR'S OFFICE. LATER.
I DON'T KNOW HOW MUCH LONGER I CAN HOLD OFF THE VOTE, MY FRIENDS.
MORE AND MORE STAR SYSTEMS ARE JOINING THE SEPARATISTS.
IF THEY DO BREAK AWAY... YOU MUST REALIZE THERE AREN'T ENOUGH JEDI TO PROTECT THE REPUBLIC. WE ARE KEEPERS OF THE PEACE, NOT SOLDIERS.
MASTER YODA, DO YOU THINK IT WILL REALLY COME TO WAR?
THE DARK SIDE CLOUDS EVERYTHING.
IMPOSSIBLE TO SEE THE FUTURE IS...
THE LOYALIST COMMITTEE HAS ARRIVED, YOUR HONOR.
SEND THEM IN.
SENATOR AMIDALA, YOUR TRAGEDY ON THE LANDING PLATFORM... TERRIBLE.
SEEING YOU ALIVE, BRINGS WARM FEELINGS TO MY HEART.

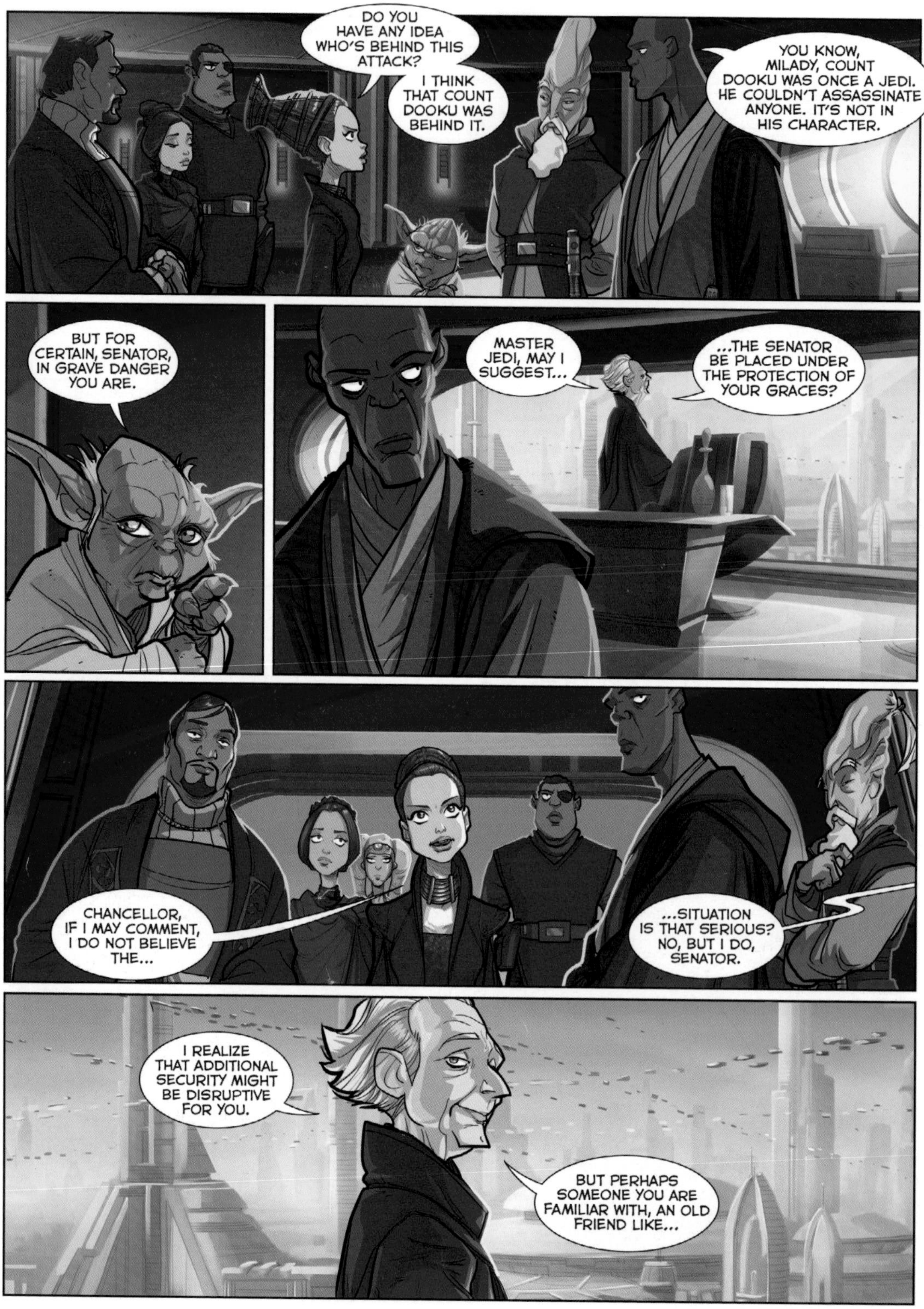
DO YOU HAVE ANY IDEA WHO'S BEHIND THIS ATTACK?
I THINK THAT COUNT DOOKU WAS BEHIND IT.
YOU KNOW, MILADY, COUNT DOOKU WAS ONCE A JEDI. HE COULDN'T ASSASSINATE ANYONE. IT'S NOT IN HIS CHARACTER.
BUT FOR CERTAIN, SENATOR, IN GRAVE DANGER YOU ARE.
MASTER JEDI, MAY I SUGGEST...
...THE SENATOR BE PLACED UNDER THE PROTECTION OF YOUR GRACES?
CHANCELLOR, IF I MAY COMMENT, I DO NOT BELIEVE THE...
...SITUATION IS THAT SERIOUS? NO, BUT I DO, SENATOR.
I REALIZE THAT ADDITIONAL SECURITY MIGHT BE DISRUPTIVE FOR YOU.
BUT PERHAPS SOMEONE YOU ARE FAMILIAR WITH, AN OLD FRIEND LIKE...

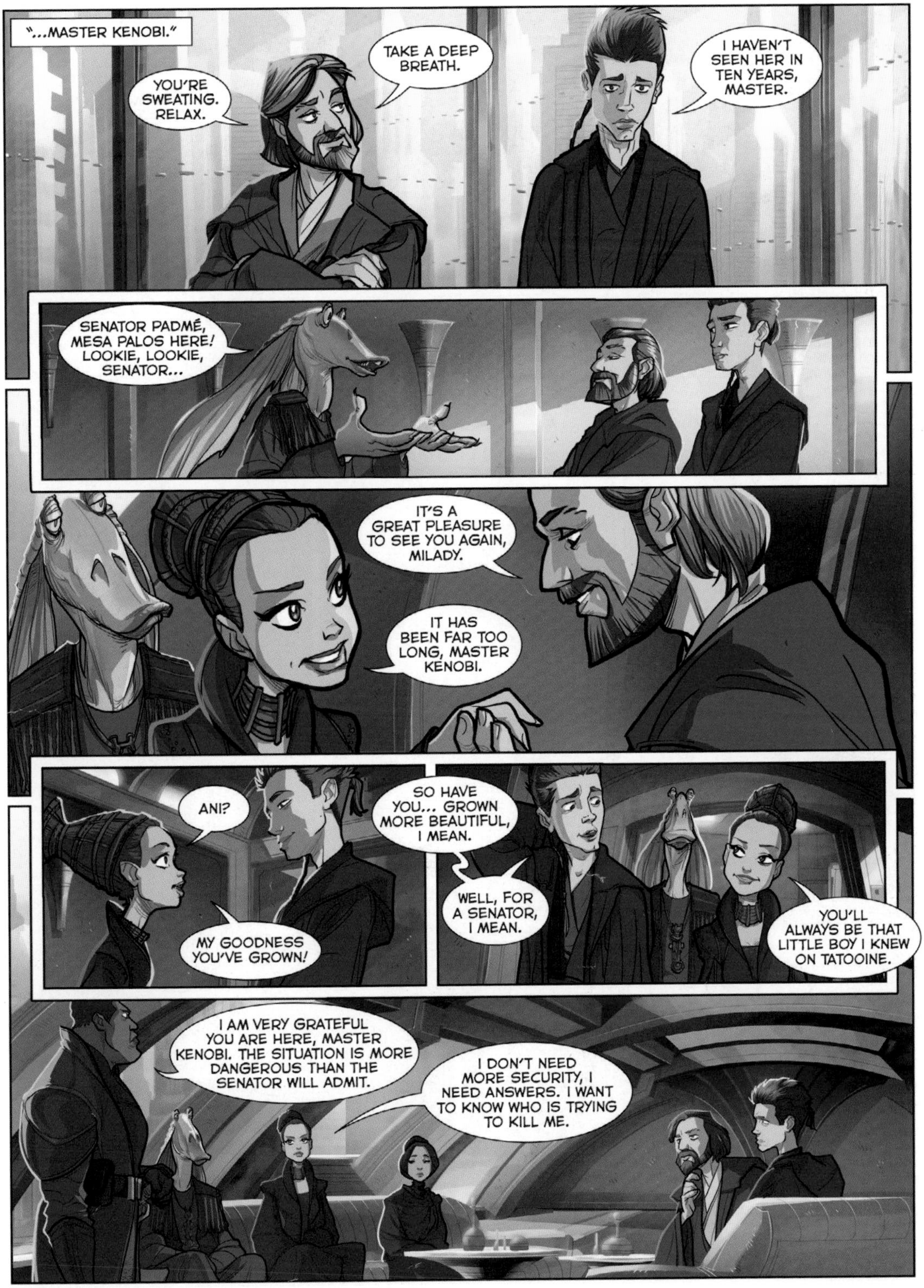
"...MASTER KENOBI."
YOU'RE SWEATING. RELAX.
TAKE A DEEP BREATH.
I HAVEN'T SEEN HER IN TEN YEARS, MASTER.
SENATOR PADMÉ, MESA PALOS HERE! LOOKIE, LOOKIE, SENATOR...
IT'S A GREAT PLEASURE TO SEE YOU AGAIN, MILADY.
IT HAS BEEN FAR TOO LONG, MASTER KENOBI.
ANI?
MY GOODNESS YOU'VE GROWN!
SO HAVE YOU... GROWN MORE BEAUTIFUL, I MEAN.
WELL, FOR A SENATOR, I MEAN.
YOU'LL ALWAYS BE THAT LITTLE BOY I KNEW ON TATOOINE.
I AM VERY GRATEFUL YOU ARE HERE, MASTER KENOBI. THE SITUATION IS MORE DANGEROUS THAN THE SENATOR WILL ADMIT.
I DON'T NEED MORE SECURITY, I NEED ANSWERS. I WANT TO KNOW WHO IS TRYING TO KILL ME.

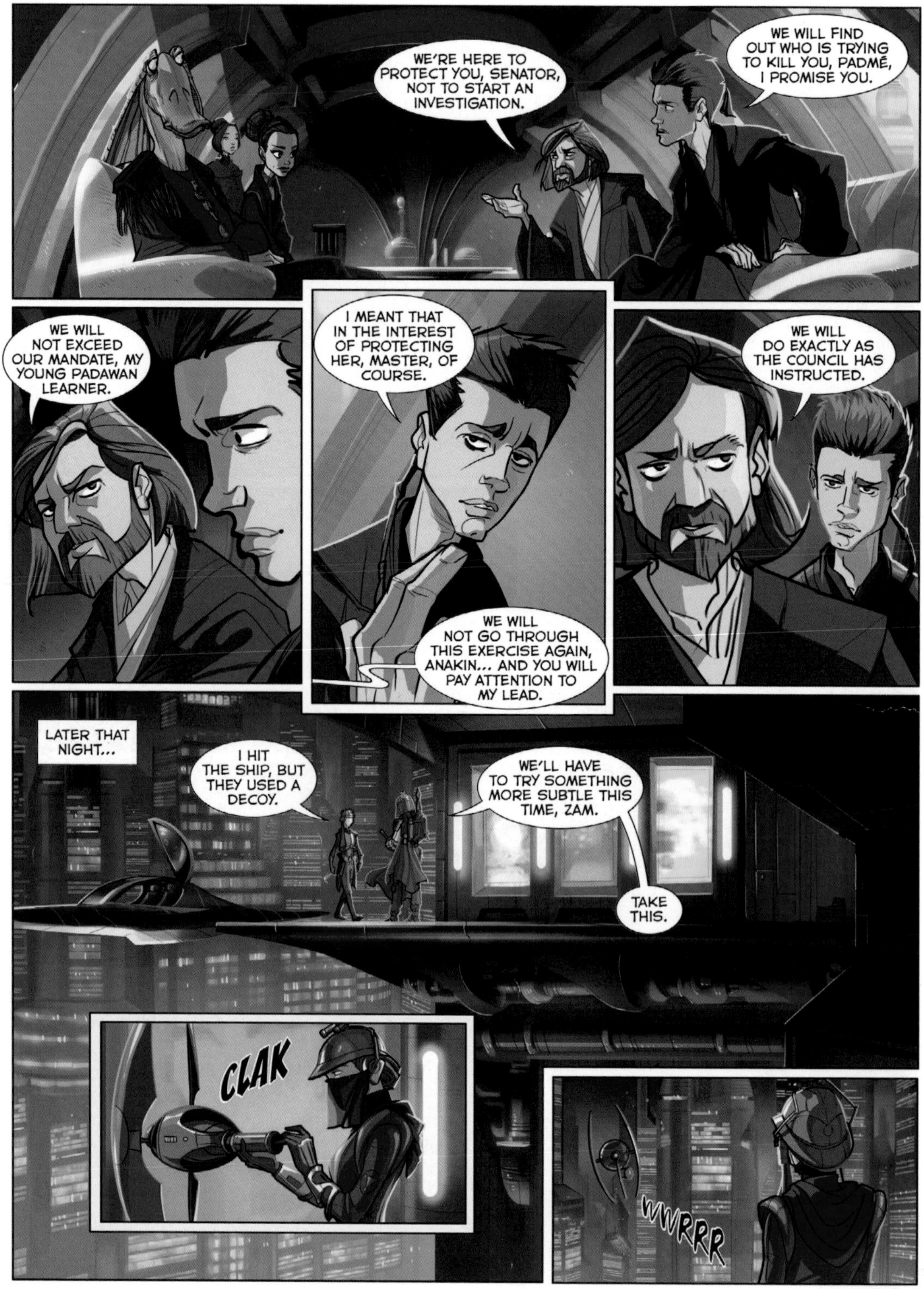
WE'RE HERE TO PROTECT YOU, SENATOR, NOT TO START AN INVESTIGATION.
WE WILL FIND OUT WHO IS TRYING TO KILL YOU, PADMÉ, I PROMISE YOU.
WE WILL NOT EXCEED OUR MANDATE, MY YOUNG PADAWAN LEARNER.
I MEANT THAT IN THE INTEREST OF PROTECTING HER, MASTER, OF COURSE.
WE WILL NOT GO THROUGH THIS EXERCISE AGAIN, ANAKIN... AND YOU WILL PAY ATTENTION TO MY LEAD.
WE WILL DO EXACTLY AS THE COUNCIL HAS INSTRUCTED.
LATER THAT NIGHT...
I HIT THE SHIP, BUT THEY USED A DECOY.
WE'LL HAVE TO TRY SOMETHING MORE SUBTLE THIS TIME, ZAM.
TAKE THIS.
CLAK
WWRRR

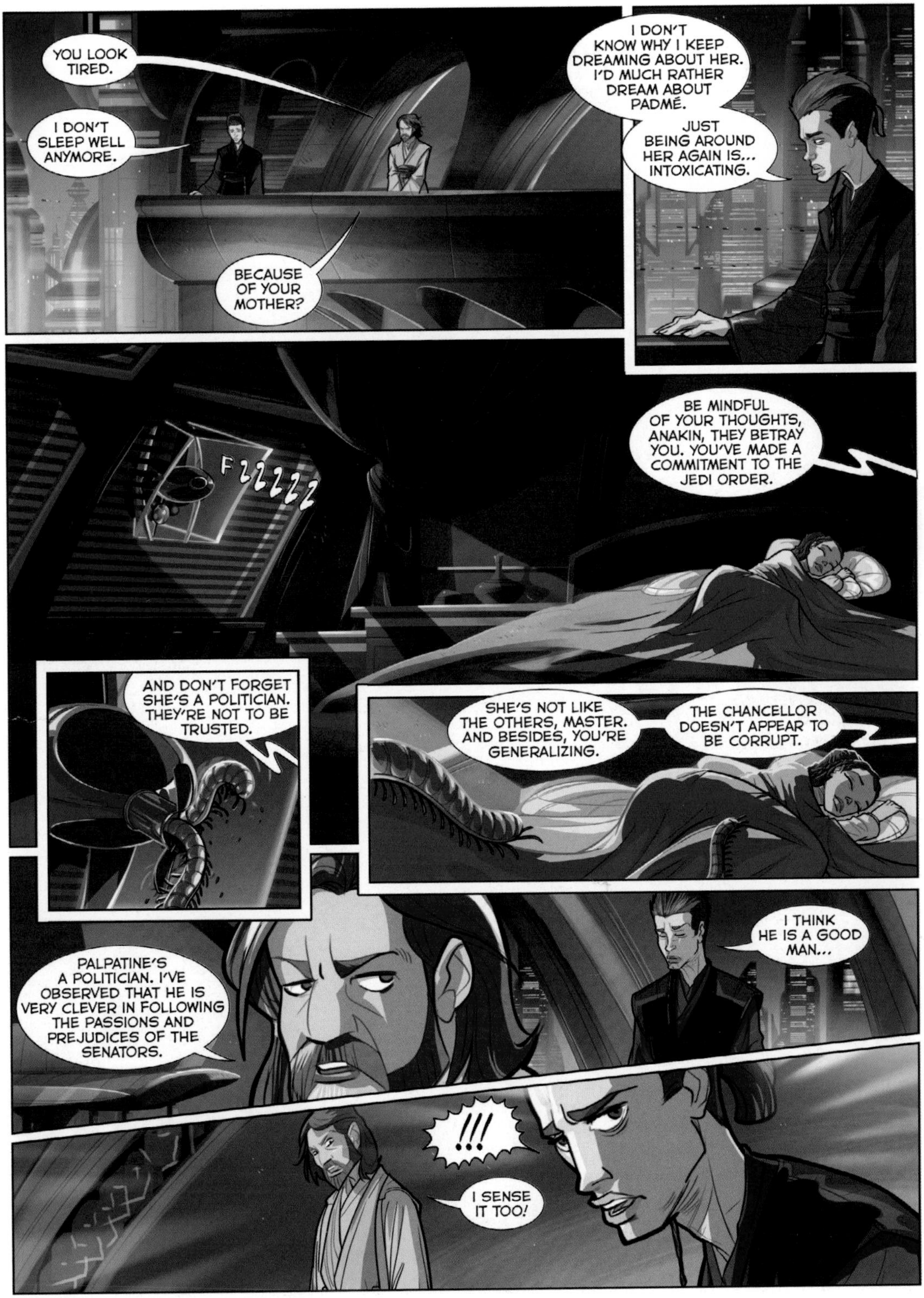
YOU LOOK TIRED.
I DON'T SLEEP WELL ANYMORE.
BECAUSE OF YOUR MOTHER?
I DON'T KNOW WHY I KEEP DREAMING ABOUT HER. I'D MUCH RATHER DREAM ABOUT PADMÉ.
JUST BEING AROUND HER AGAIN IS... INTOXICATING.
BE MINDFUL OF YOUR THOUGHTS, ANAKIN, THEY BETRAY YOU. YOU'VE MADE A COMMITMENT TO THE JEDI ORDER.
FZZZZZZ
AND DON'T FORGET SHE'S A POLITICIAN. THEY'RE NOT TO BE TRUSTED.
SHE'S NOT LIKE THE OTHERS, MASTER. AND BESIDES, YOU'RE GENERALIZING.
THE CHANCELLOR DOESN'T APPEAR TO BE CORRUPT.
PALPATINE'S A POLITICIAN. I'VE OBSERVED THAT HE IS VERY CLEVER IN FOLLOWING THE PASSIONS AND PREJUDICES OF THE SENATORS.
I THINK HE IS A GOOD MAN...
!!!
I SENSE IT TOO!

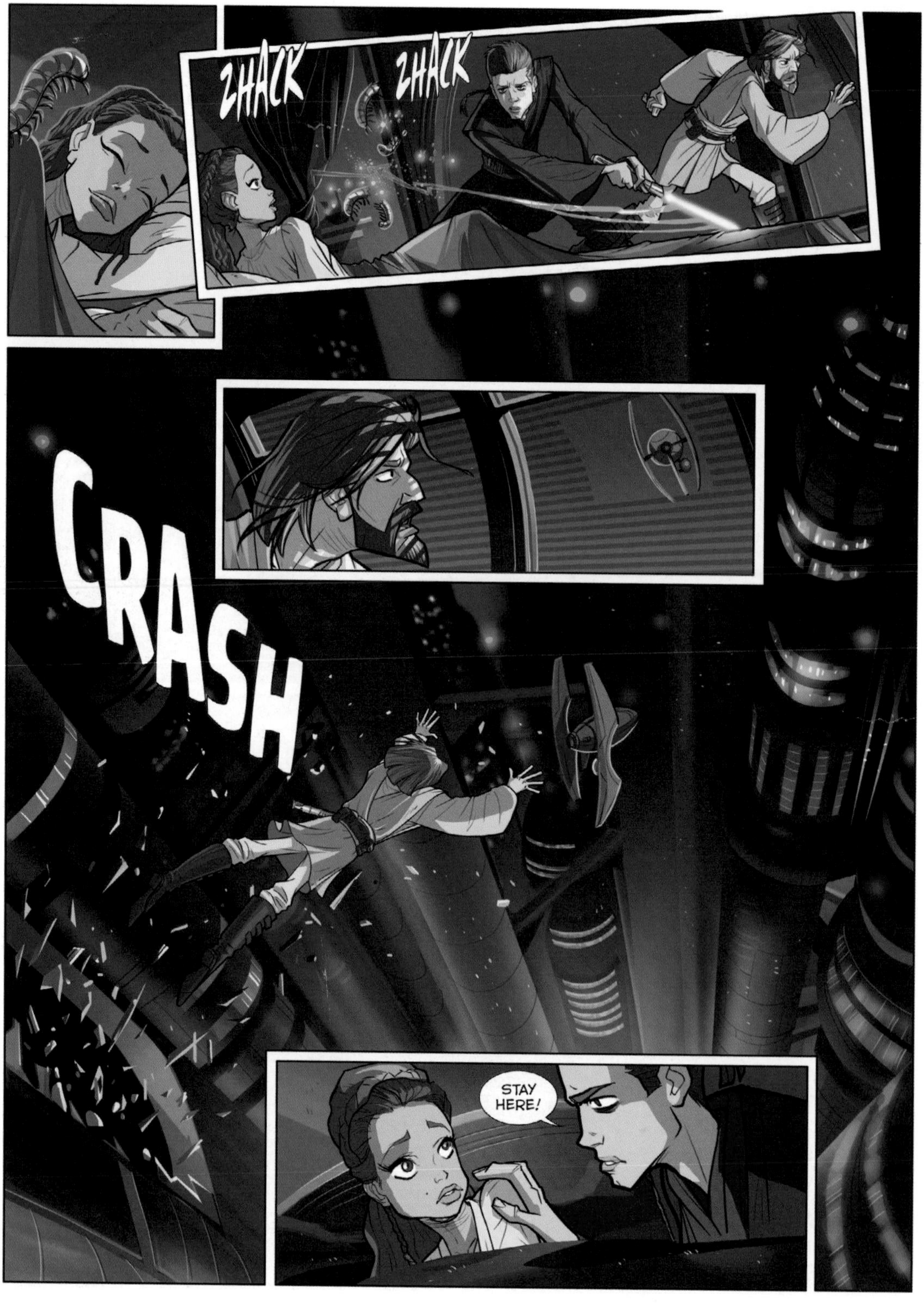

ZHACK
ZHACK
CRASH
STAY HERE!

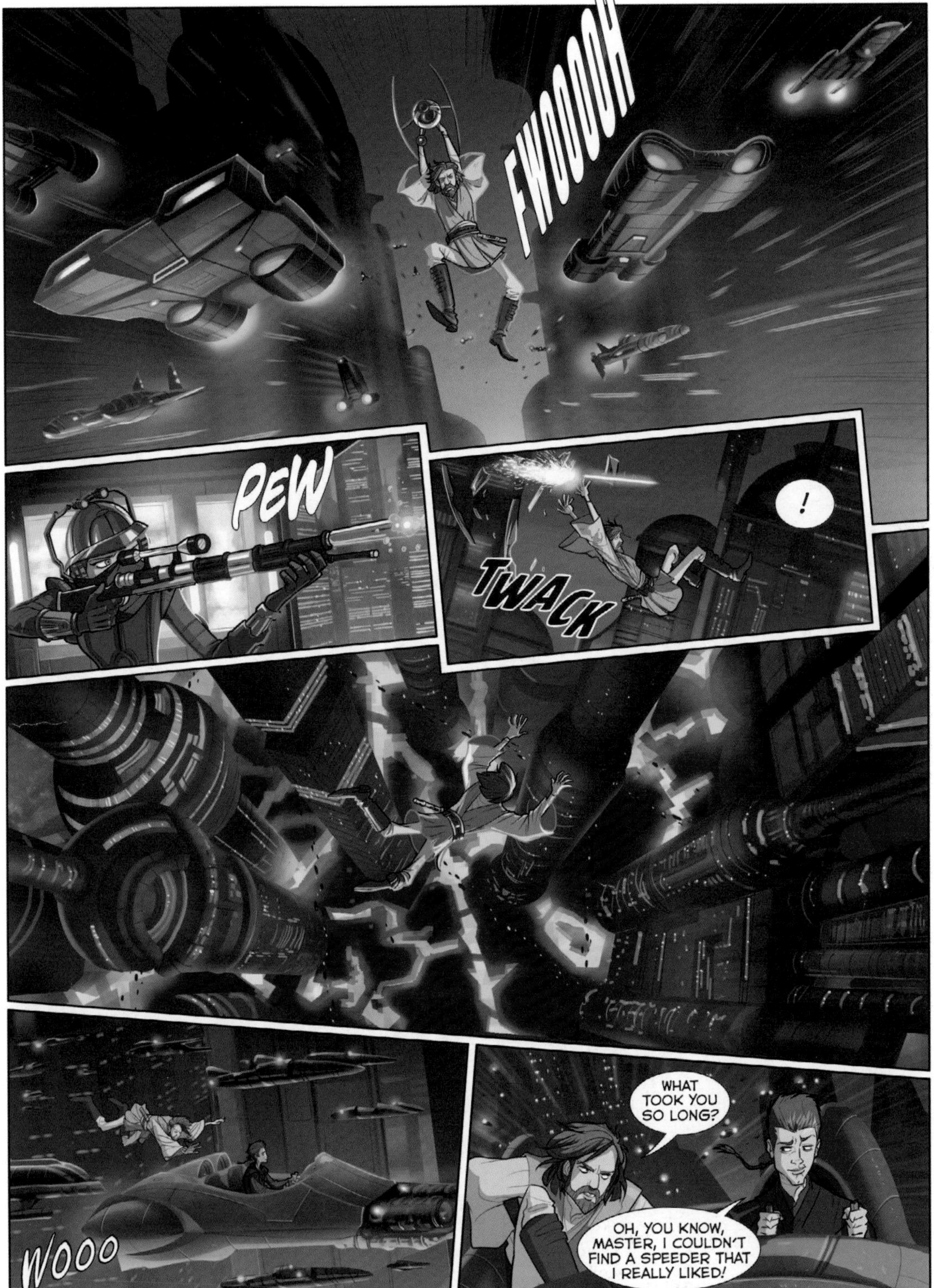
FWOOOSH
PEW
!
TWACK
WOOO
WHAT TOOK YOU SO LONG?
OH, YOU KNOW, MASTER, I COULDN'T FIND A SPEEDER THAT I REALLY LIKED!

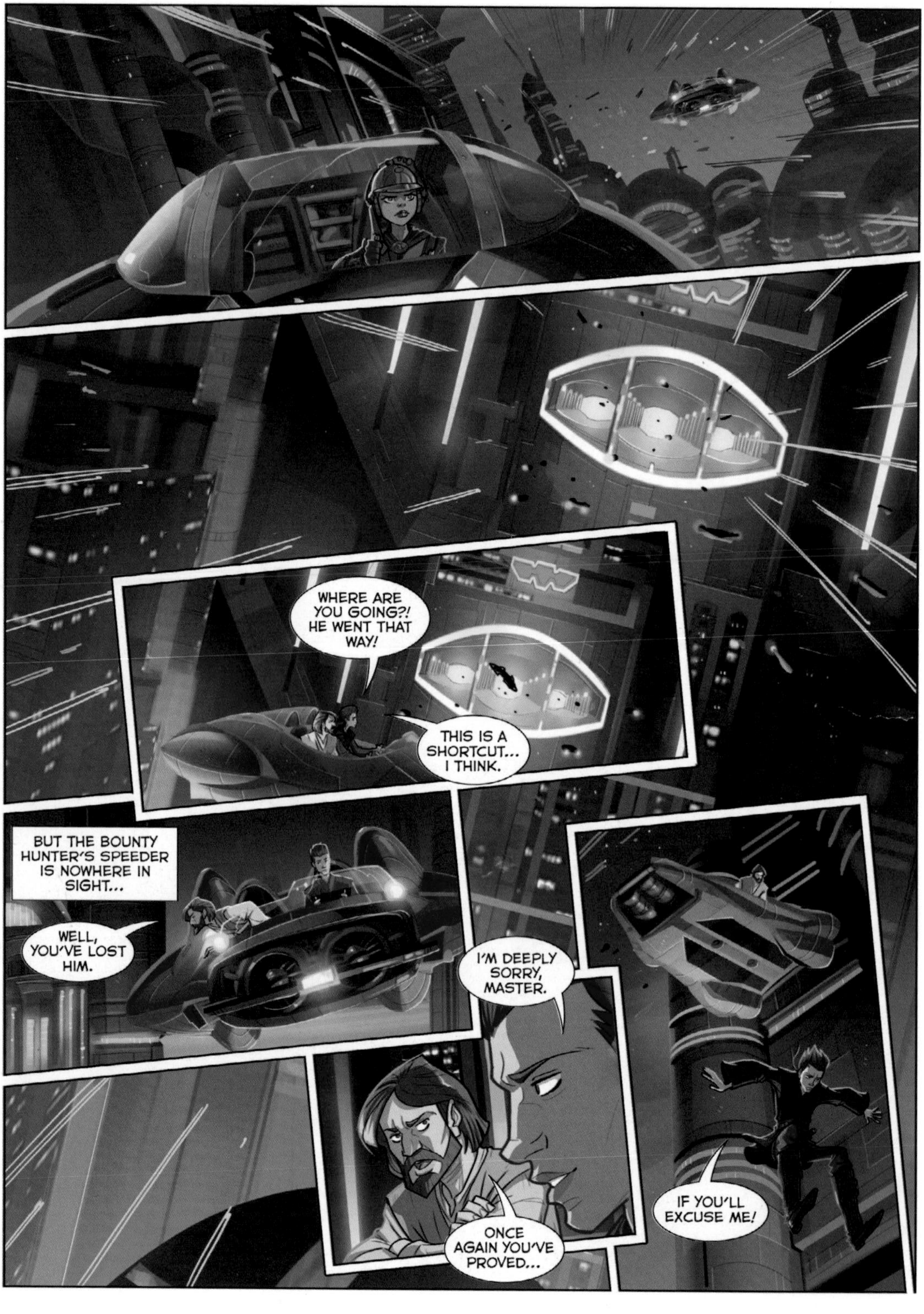
WHERE ARE YOU GOING?! HE WENT THAT WAY!
THIS IS A SHORTCUT... I THINK.
BUT THE BOUNTY HUNTER'S SPEEDER IS NOWHERE IN SIGHT...
WELL, YOU'VE LOST HIM.
I'M DEEPLY SORRY, MASTER.
ONCE AGAIN YOU'VE PROVED...
IF YOU'LL EXCUSE ME!

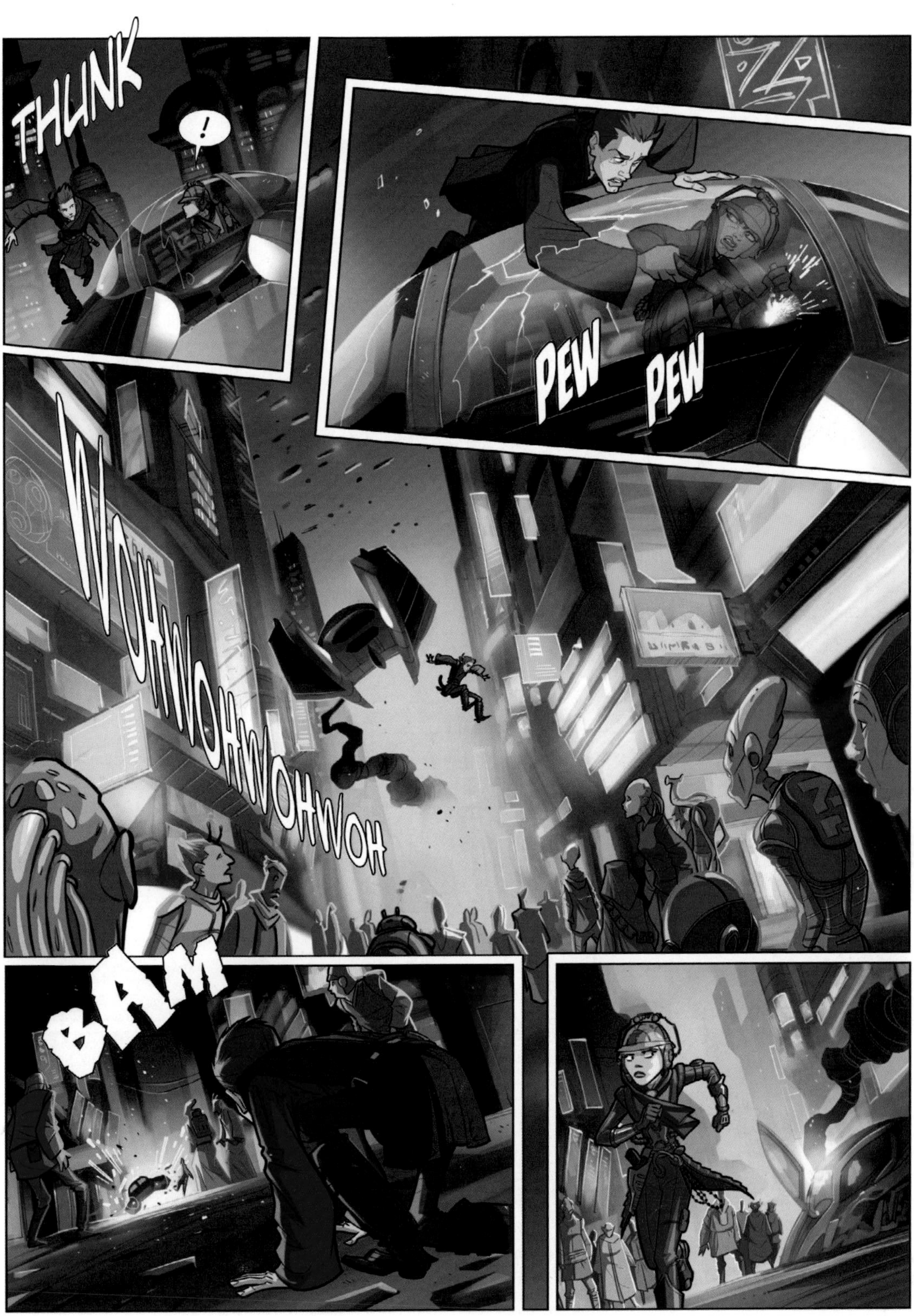
THUNK
!
PEW
PEW
WOHWOHWOHWOHWOHWOH
BAM

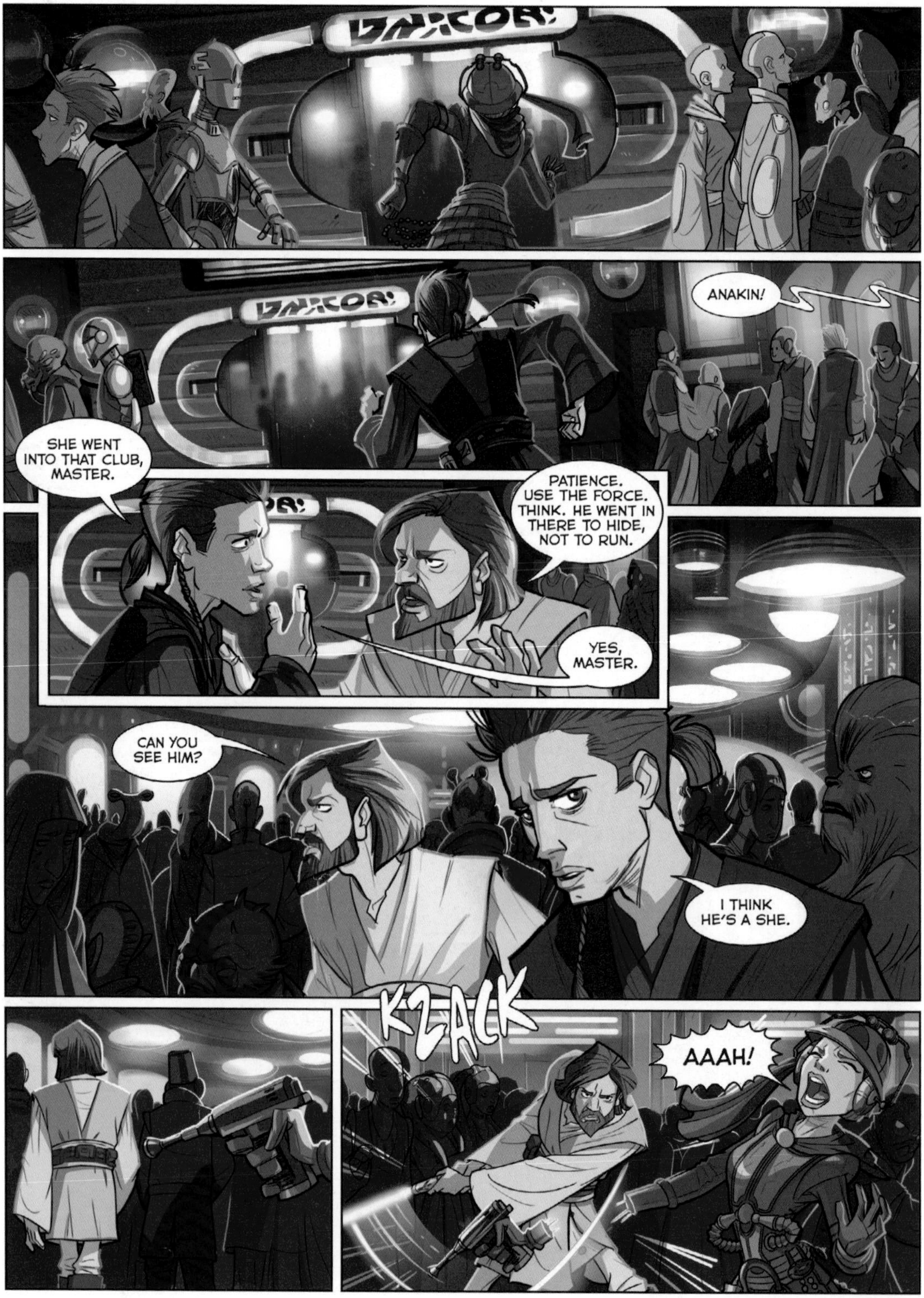
ANAKIN!
SHE WENT INTO THAT CLUB, MASTER.
PATIENCE. USE THE FORCE. THINK. HE WENT IN THERE TO HIDE, NOT TO RUN.
YES, MASTER.
CAN YOU SEE HIM?
I THINK HE'S A SHE.
KZACK
AAAH!

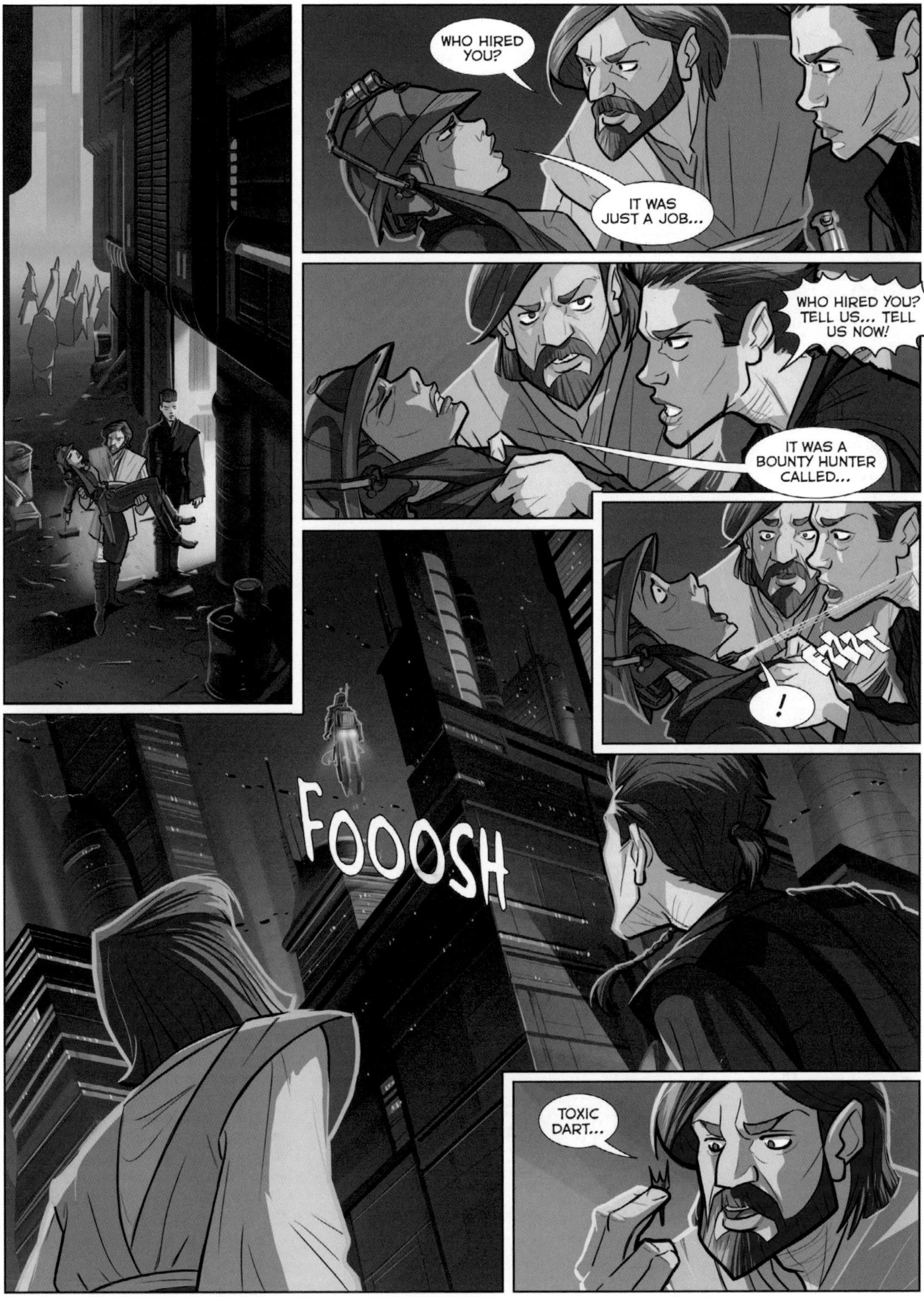
WHO HIRED YOU?
IT WAS JUST A JOB...
WHO HIRED YOU? TELL US... TELL US NOW!
IT WAS A BOUNTY HUNTER CALLED...
!
FOOOSH
TOXIC DART...

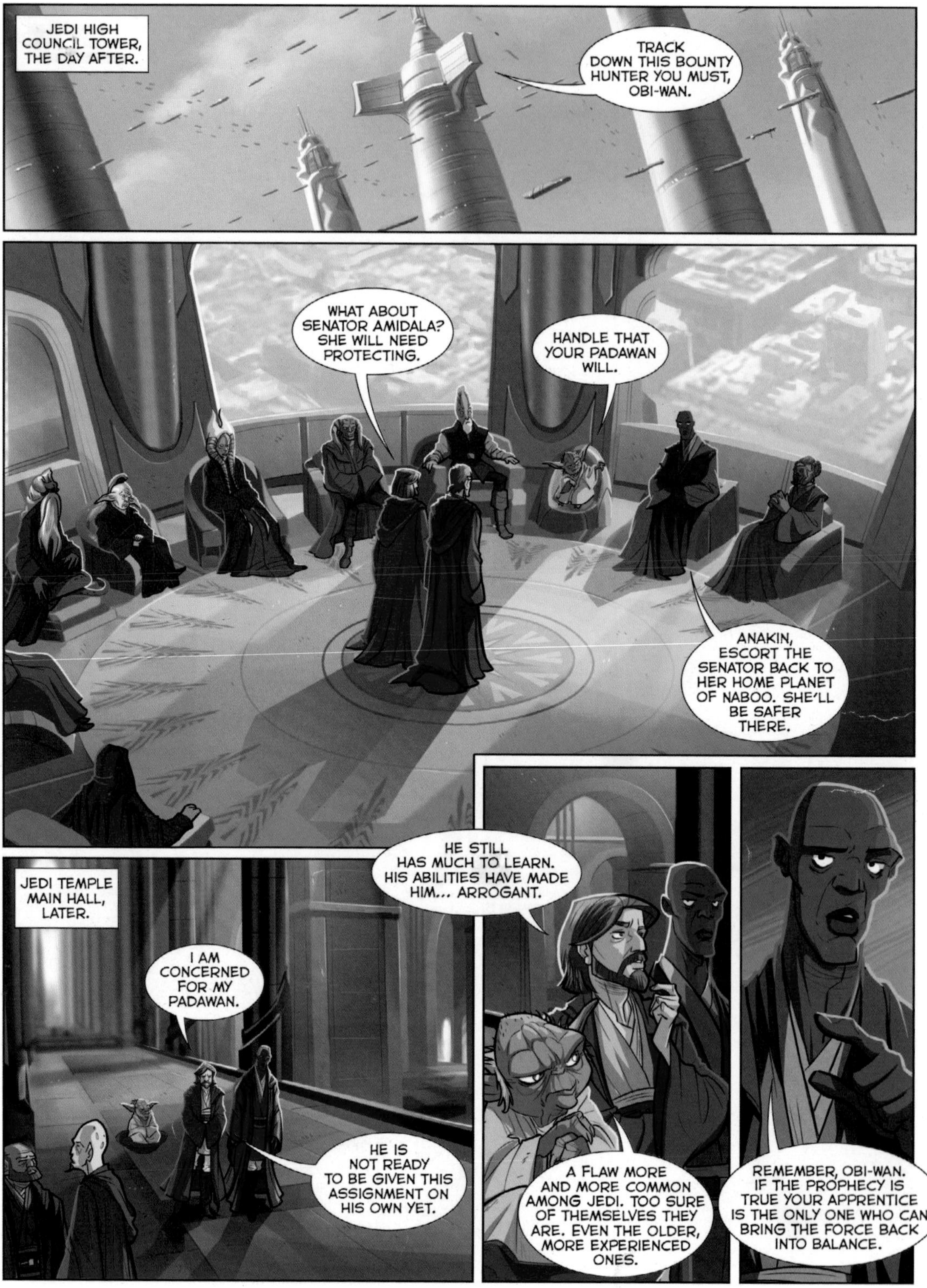

JEDI HIGH COUNCIL TOWER, THE DAY AFTER.
TRACK DOWN THIS BOUNTY HUNTER YOU MUST, OBI-WAN.
WHAT ABOUT SENATOR AMIDALA? SHE WILL NEED PROTECTING.
HANDLE THAT YOUR PADAWAN WILL.
ANAKIN, ESCORT THE SENATOR BACK TO HER HOME PLANET OF NABOO. SHE'LL BE SAFER THERE.
JEDI TEMPLE MAIN HALL, LATER.
I AM CONCERNED FOR MY PADAWAN.
HE IS NOT READY TO BE GIVEN THIS ASSIGNMENT ON HIS OWN YET.
HE STILL HAS MUCH TO LEARN. HIS ABILITIES HAVE MADE HIM... ARROGANT.
A FLAW MORE AND MORE COMMON AMONG JEDI. TOO SURE OF THEMSELVES THEY ARE. EVEN THE OLDER, MORE EXPERIENCED ONES.
REMEMBER, OBI-WAN. IF THE PROPHECY IS TRUE YOUR APPRENTICE IS THE ONLY ONE WHO CAN BRING THE FORCE BACK INTO BALANCE.

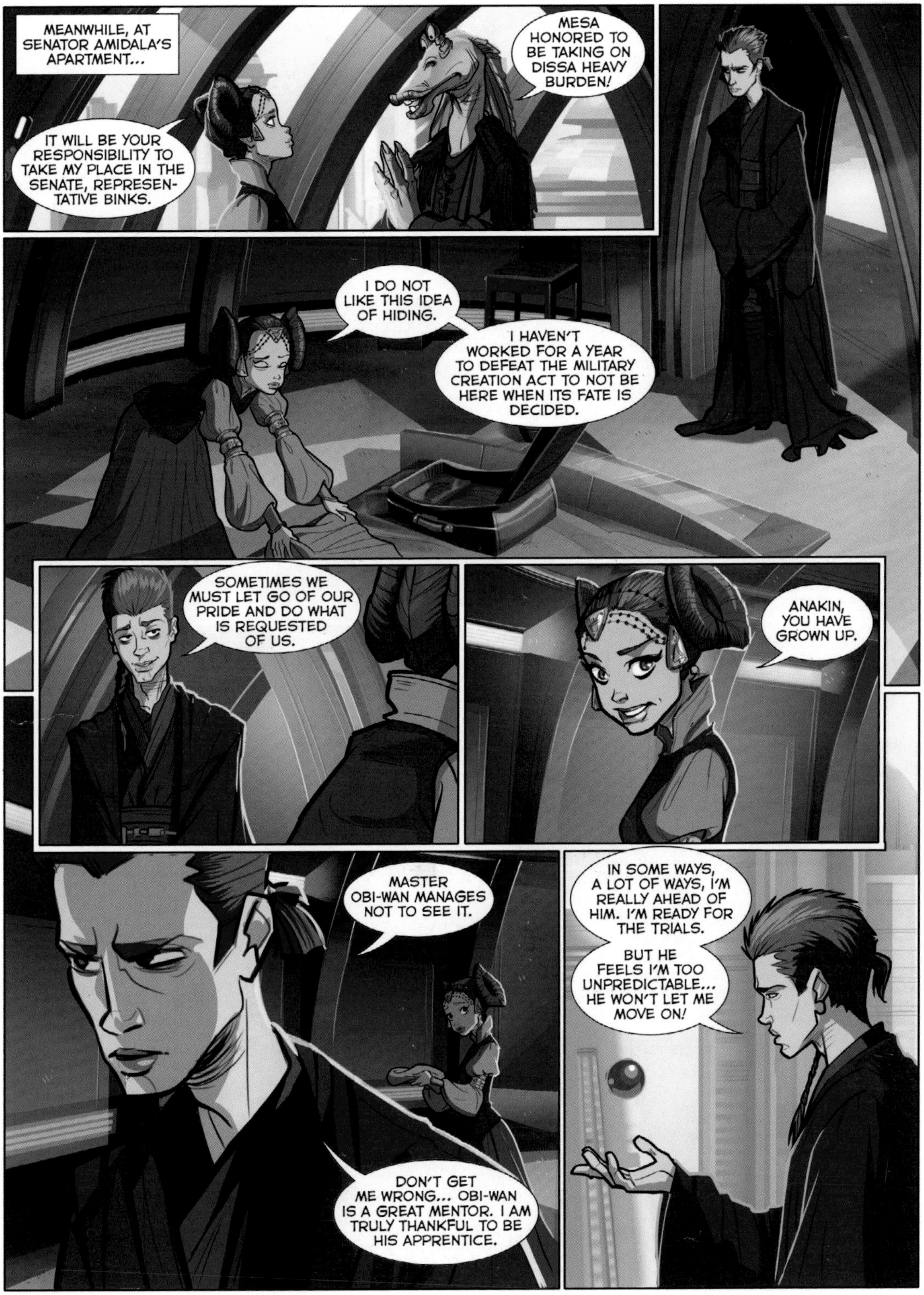

MEANWHILE, AT SENATOR AMIDALA'S APARTMENT...
IT WILL BE YOUR RESPONSIBILITY TO TAKE MY PLACE IN THE SENATE, REPRESENTATIVE BINKS.
MESA HONORED TO BE TAKING ON DISSA HEAVY BURDEN!
I DO NOT LIKE THIS IDEA OF HIDING.
I HAVEN'T WORKED FOR A YEAR TO DEFEAT THE MILITARY CREATION ACT TO NOT BE HERE WHEN ITS FATE IS DECIDED.
SOMETIMES WE MUST LET GO OF OUR PRIDE AND DO WHAT IS REQUESTED OF US.
ANAKIN, YOU HAVE GROWN UP.
MASTER OBI-WAN MANAGES NOT TO SEE IT.
DON'T GET ME WRONG... OBI-WAN IS A GREAT MENTOR. I AM TRULY THANKFUL TO BE HIS APPRENTICE.
IN SOME WAYS, A LOT OF WAYS, I'M REALLY AHEAD OF HIM. I'M READY FOR THE TRIALS.
BUT HE FEELS I'M TOO UNPREDICTABLE... HE WON'T LET ME MOVE ON!

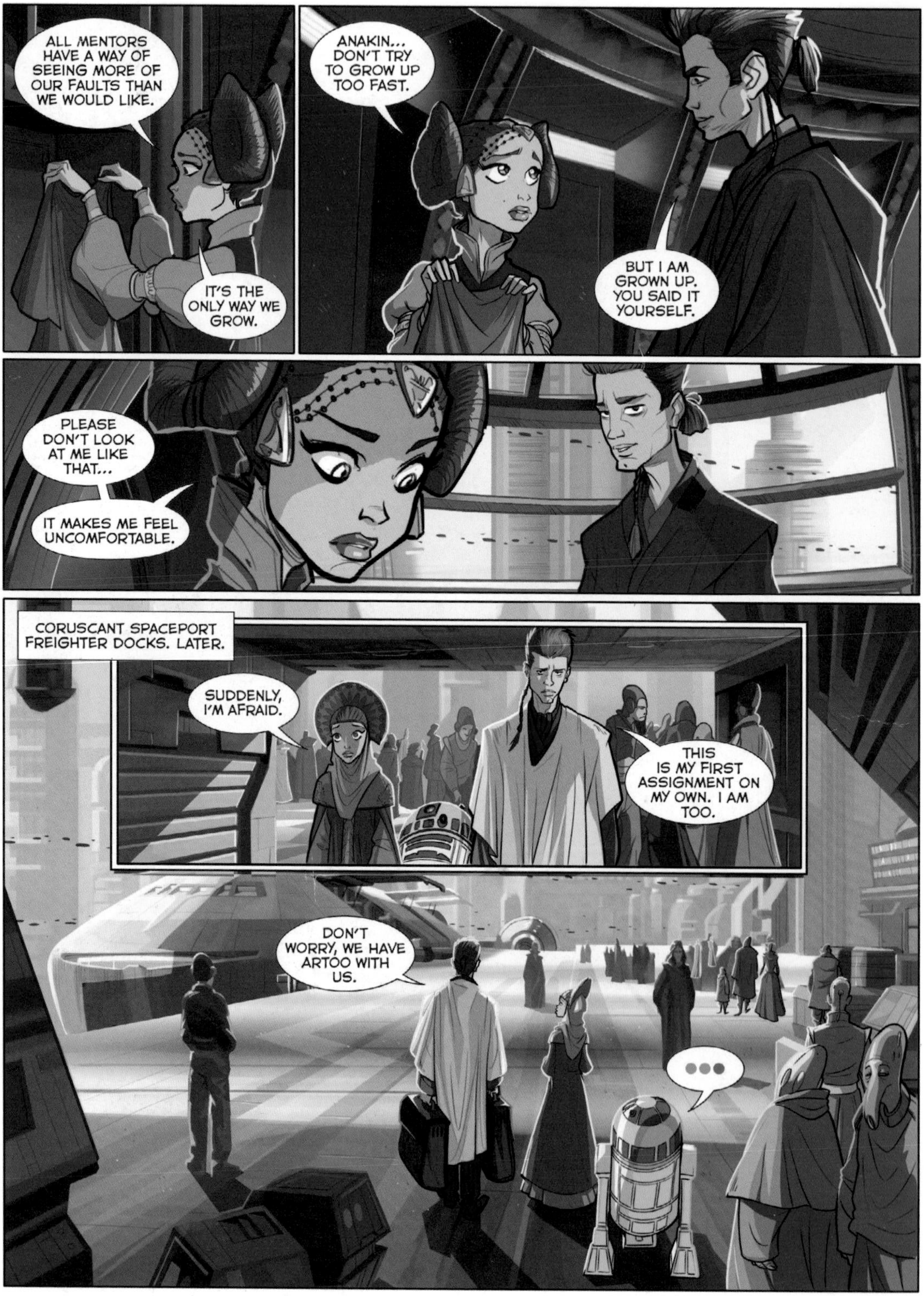
ALL MENTORS HAVE A WAY OF SEEING MORE OF OUR FAULTS THAN WE WOULD LIKE.
IT'S THE ONLY WAY WE GROW.
ANAKIN... DON'T TRY TO GROW UP TOO FAST.
BUT I AM GROWN UP. YOU SAID IT YOURSELF.
PLEASE DON'T LOOK AT ME LIKE THAT...
IT MAKES ME FEEL UNCOMFORTABLE.
CORUSCANT SPACEPORT FREIGHTER DOCKS. LATER.
SUDDENLY, I'M AFRAID.
THIS IS MY FIRST ASSIGNMENT ON MY OWN. I AM TOO.
DON'T WORRY, WE HAVE ARTOO WITH US.
•••

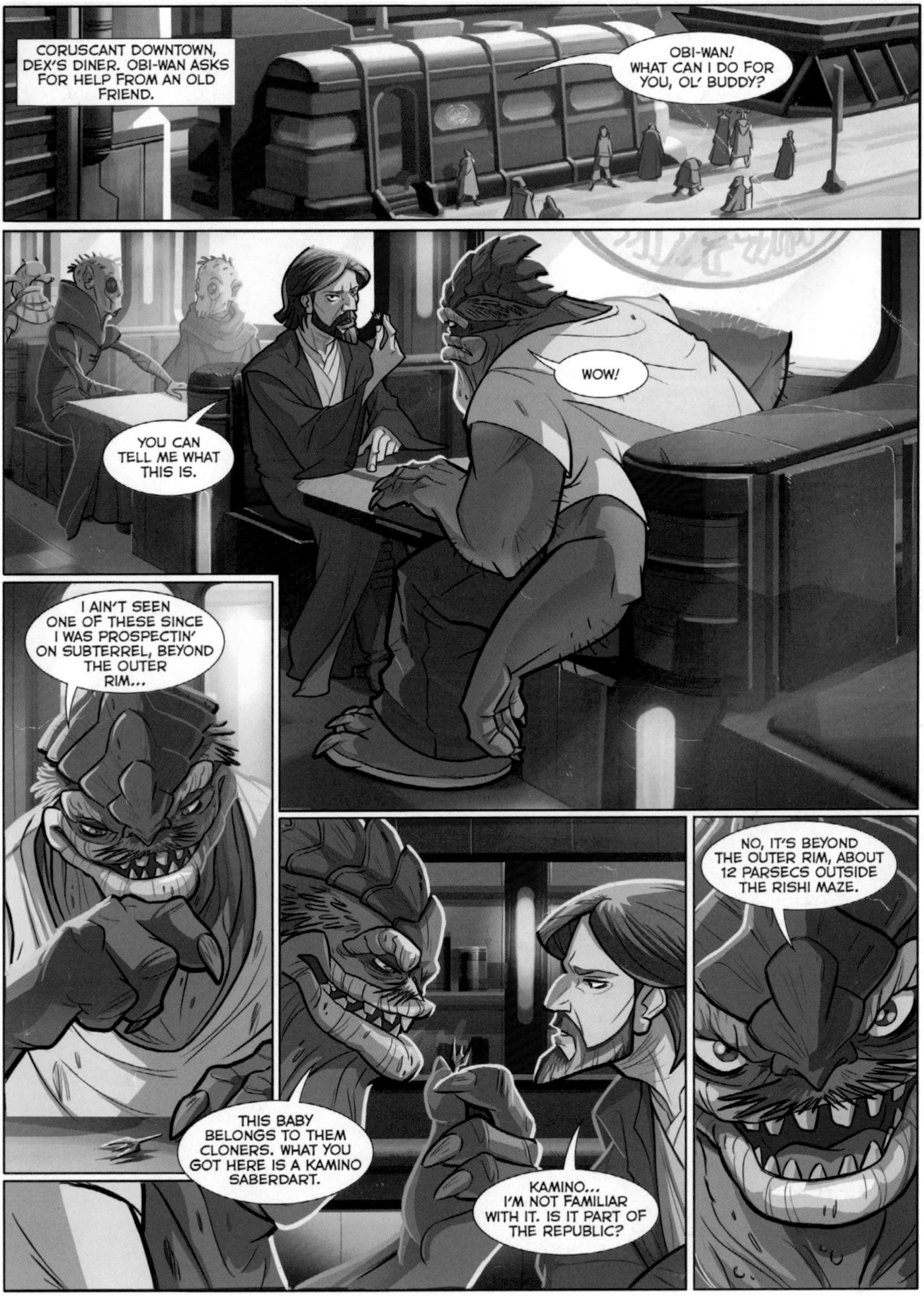
CORUSCANT DOWNTOWN, DEX'S DINER. OBI-WAN ASKS FOR HELP FROM AN OLD FRIEND.
OBI-WAN! WHAT CAN I DO FOR YOU, OL' BUDDY?
WOW!
YOU CAN TELL ME WHAT THIS IS.
I AIN'T SEEN ONE OF THESE SINCE I WAS PROSPECTIN' ON SUBTERREL, BEYOND THE OUTER RIM...
THIS BABY BELONGS TO THEM CLONERS. WHAT YOU GOT HERE IS A KAMINO SABERDART.
KAMINO... I'M NOT FAMILIAR WITH IT. IS IT PART OF THE REPUBLIC?
NO, IT'S BEYOND THE OUTER RIM, ABOUT 12 PARSECS OUTSIDE THE RISHI MAZE.

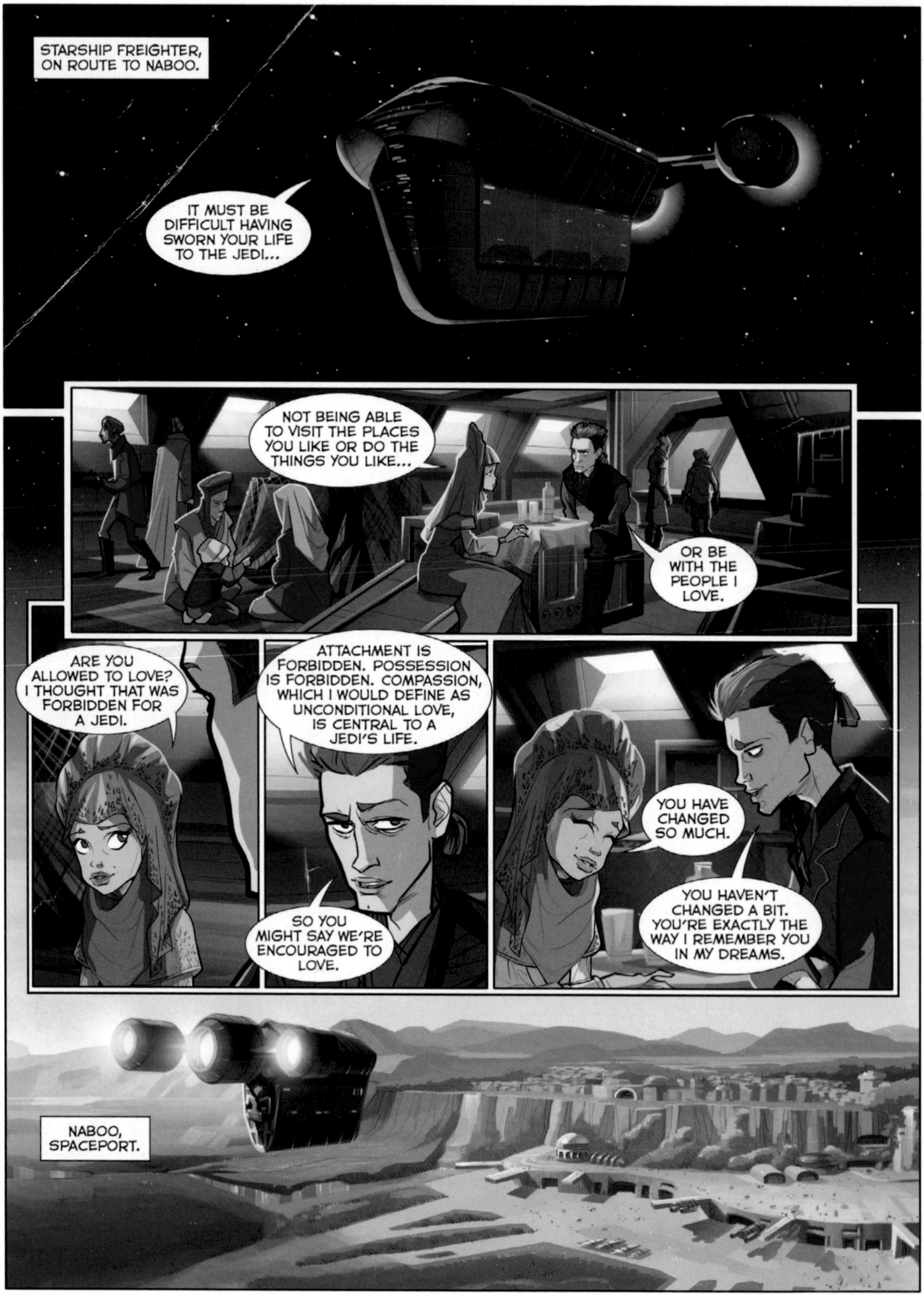
STARSHIP FREIGHTER, ON ROUTE TO NABOO.
IT MUST BE DIFFICULT HAVING SWORN YOUR LIFE TO THE JEDI...
NOT BEING ABLE TO VISIT THE PLACES YOU LIKE OR DO THE THINGS YOU LIKE...
OR BE WITH THE PEOPLE I LOVE.
ARE YOU ALLOWED TO LOVE? I THOUGHT THAT WAS FORBIDDEN FOR A JEDI.
ATTACHMENT IS FORBIDDEN. POSSESSION IS FORBIDDEN. COMPASSION, WHICH I WOULD DEFINE AS UNCONDITIONAL LOVE, IS CENTRAL TO A JEDI'S LIFE.
SO YOU MIGHT SAY WE'RE ENCOURAGED TO LOVE.
YOU HAVE CHANGED SO MUCH.
YOU HAVEN'T CHANGED A BIT. YOU'RE EXACTLY THE WAY I REMEMBER YOU IN MY DREAMS.
NABOO, SPACEPORT.

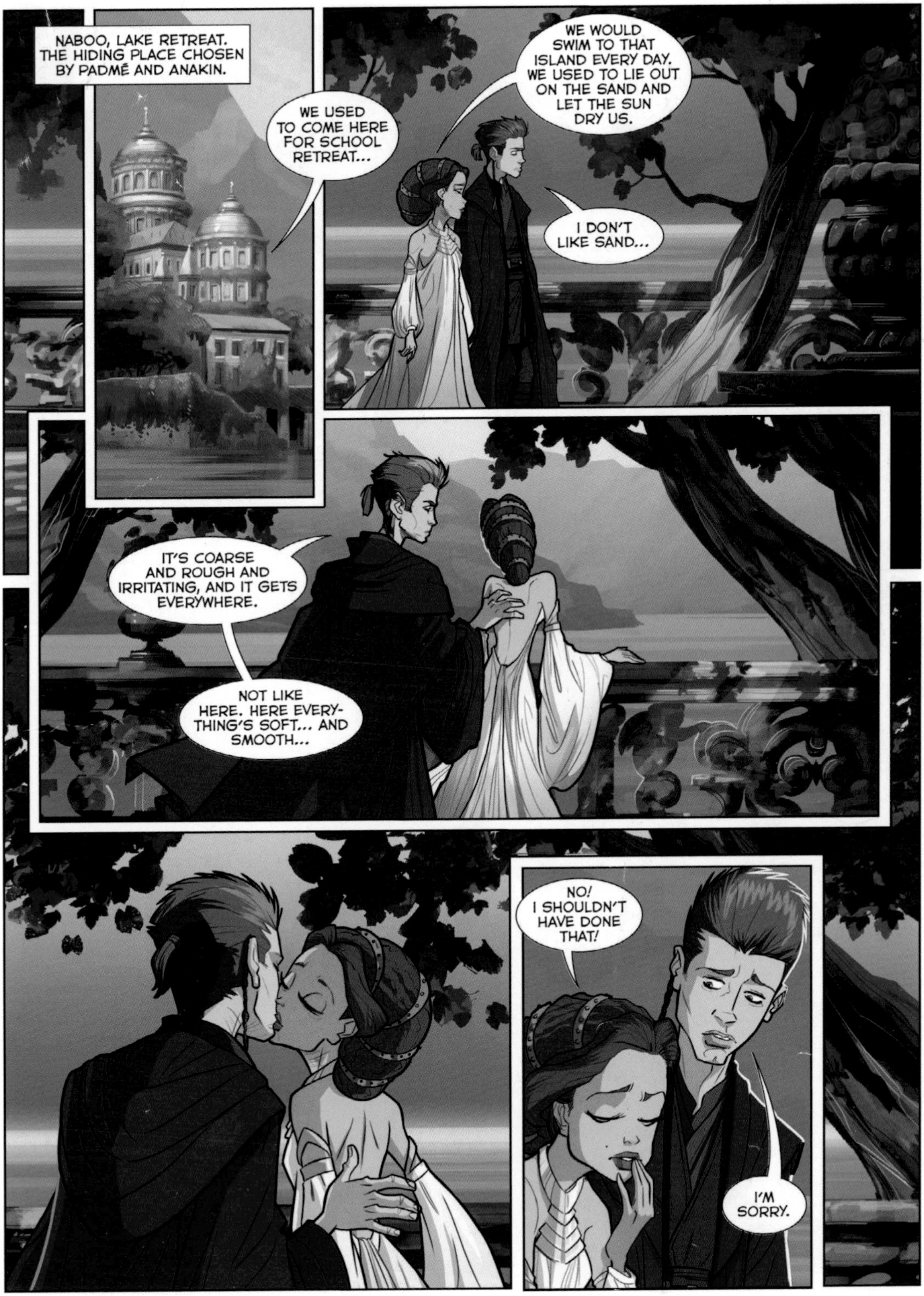
NABOO, LAKE RETREAT. THE HIDING PLACE CHOSEN BY PADMÉ AND ANAKIN.
WE USED TO COME HERE FOR SCHOOL RETREAT...
WE WOULD SWIM TO THAT ISLAND EVERY DAY. WE USED TO LIE OUT ON THE SAND AND LET THE SUN DRY US.
I DON'T LIKE SAND...
IT'S COARSE AND ROUGH AND IRRITATING, AND IT GETS EVERYWHERE.
NOT LIKE HERE. HERE EVERY-THING'S SOFT... AND SMOOTH...
NO! I SHOULDN'T HAVE DONE THAT!
I'M SORRY.

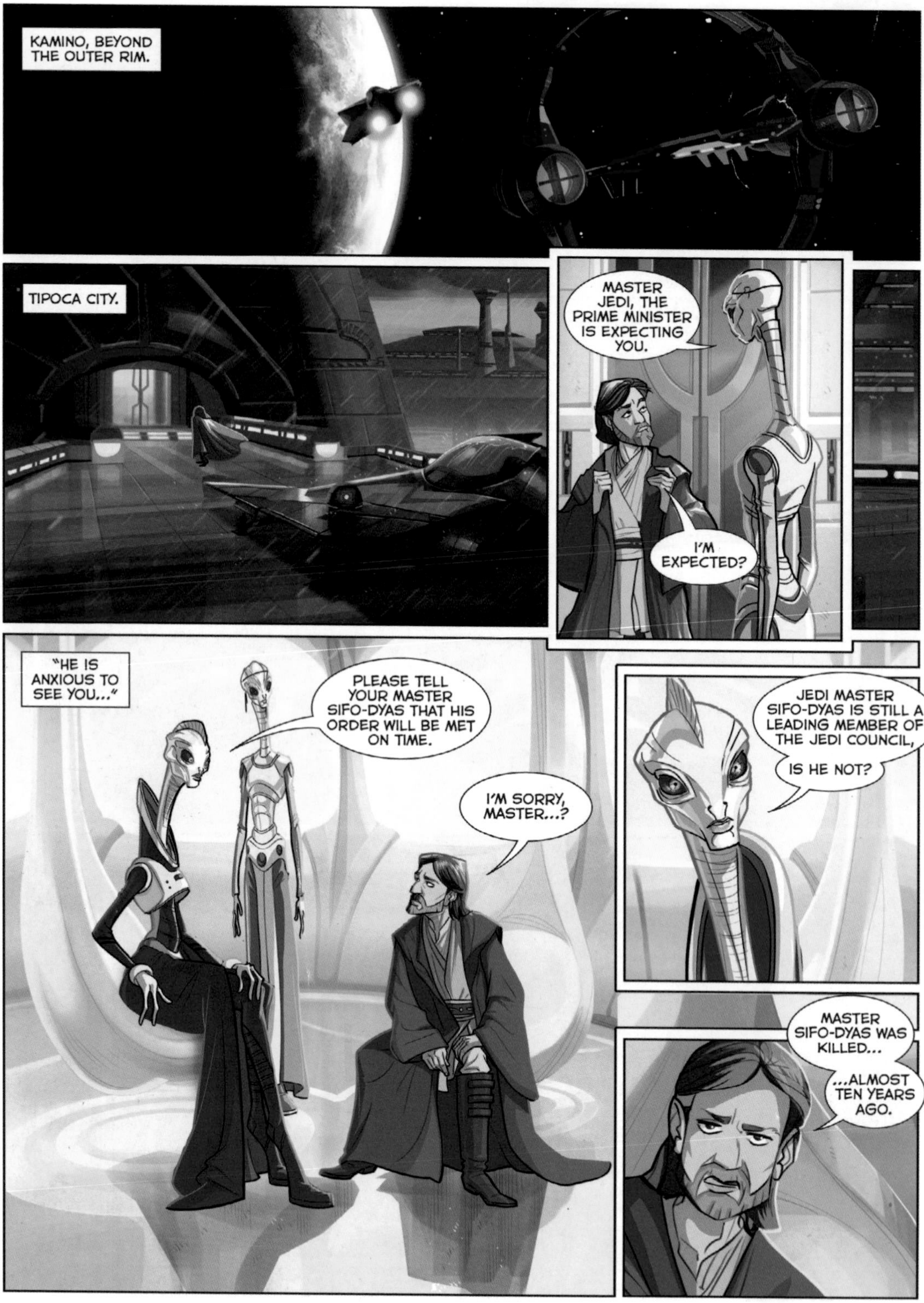

KAMINO, BEYOND THE OUTER RIM.
TIPOCA CITY.
MASTER JEDI, THE PRIME MINISTER IS EXPECTING YOU.
I'M EXPECTED?
"HE IS ANXIOUS TO SEE YOU..."
PLEASE TELL YOUR MASTER SIFO-DYAS THAT HIS ORDER WILL BE MET ON TIME.
I'M SORRY, MASTER...?
JEDI MASTER SIFO-DYAS IS STILL A LEADING MEMBER OF THE JEDI COUNCIL,
IS HE NOT?
MASTER SIFO-DYAS WAS KILLED...
...ALMOST TEN YEARS AGO.

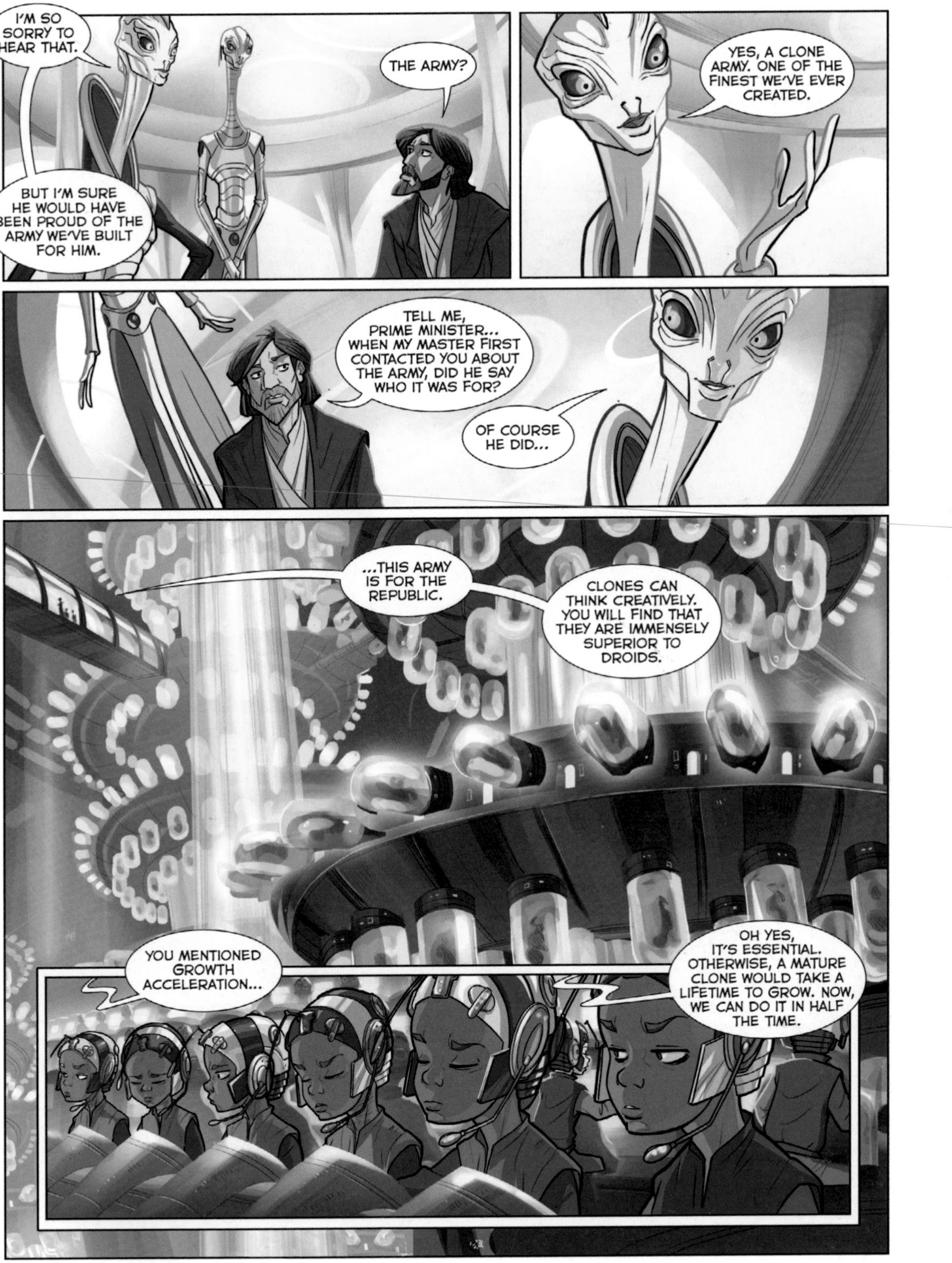

I'M SO SORRY TO HEAR THAT.
BUT I'M SURE HE WOULD HAVE BEEN PROUD OF THE ARMY WE'VE BUILT FOR HIM.
THE ARMY?
YES, A CLONE ARMY. ONE OF THE FINEST WE'VE EVER CREATED.
TELL ME, PRIME MINISTER... WHEN MY MASTER FIRST CONTACTED YOU ABOUT THE ARMY, DID HE SAY WHO IT WAS FOR?
OF COURSE HE DID...
...THIS ARMY IS FOR THE REPUBLIC.
CLONES CAN THINK CREATIVELY. YOU WILL FIND THAT THEY ARE IMMENSELY SUPERIOR TO DROIDS.
YOU MENTIONED GROWTH ACCELERATION...
OH YES, IT'S ESSENTIAL. OTHERWISE, A MATURE CLONE WOULD TAKE A LIFETIME TO GROW. NOW, WE CAN DO IT IN HALF THE TIME.

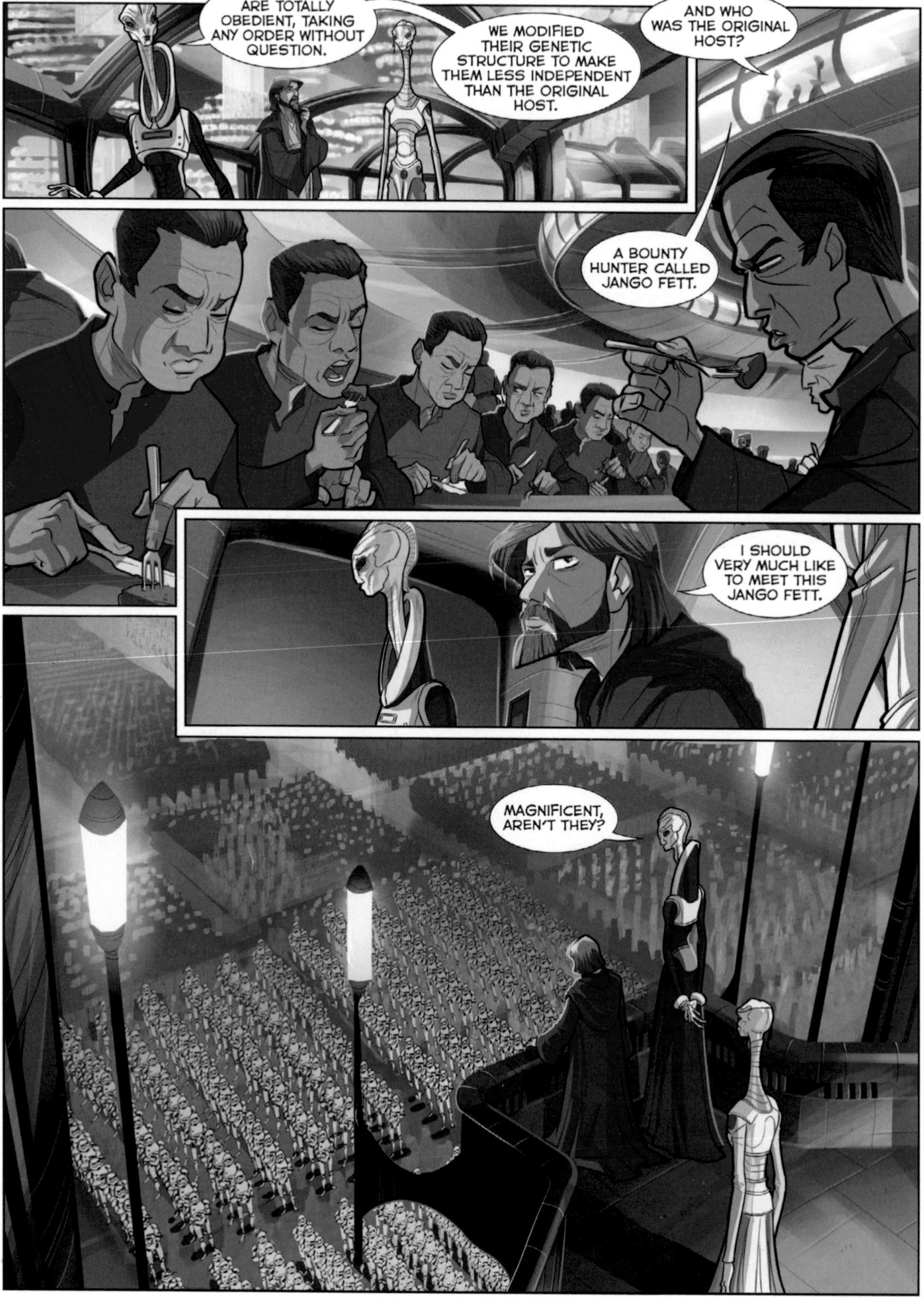
THEY ARE TOTALLY OBEDIENT, TAKING ANY ORDER WITHOUT QUESTION.
WE MODIFIED THEIR GENETIC STRUCTURE TO MAKE THEM LESS INDEPENDENT THAN THE ORIGINAL HOST.
AND WHO WAS THE ORIGINAL HOST?
A BOUNTY HUNTER CALLED JANGO FETT.
I SHOULD VERY MUCH LIKE TO MEET THIS JANGO FETT.
MAGNIFICENT, AREN'T THEY?

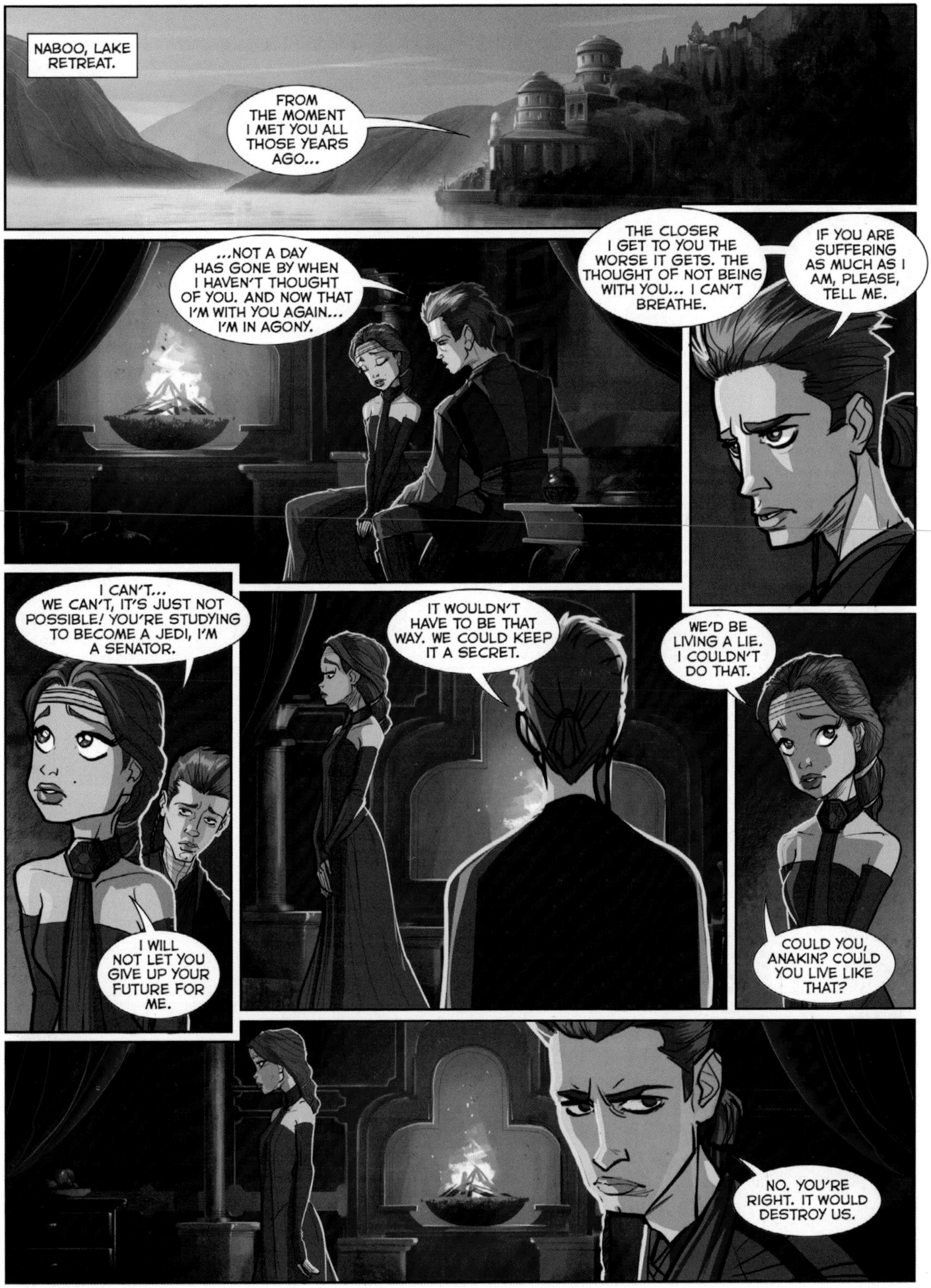
NABOO, LAKE RETREAT.
FROM THE MOMENT I MET YOU ALL THOSE YEARS AGO...
...NOT A DAY HAS GONE BY WHEN I HAVEN'T THOUGHT OF YOU. AND NOW THAT I'M WITH YOU AGAIN... I'M IN AGONY.
THE CLOSER I GET TO YOU THE WORSE IT GETS. THE THOUGHT OF NOT BEING WITH YOU... I CAN'T BREATHE.
IF YOU ARE SUFFERING AS MUCH AS I AM, PLEASE, TELL ME.
I CAN'T... WE CAN'T, IT'S JUST NOT POSSIBLE! YOU'RE STUDYING TO BECOME A JEDI, I'M A SENATOR.
I WILL NOT LET YOU GIVE UP YOUR FUTURE FOR ME.
IT WOULDN'T HAVE TO BE THAT WAY. WE COULD KEEP IT A SECRET.
WE'D BE LIVING A LIE. I COULDN'T DO THAT.
COULD YOU, ANAKIN? COULD YOU LIVE LIKE THAT?
NO. YOU'RE RIGHT. IT WOULD DESTROY US.

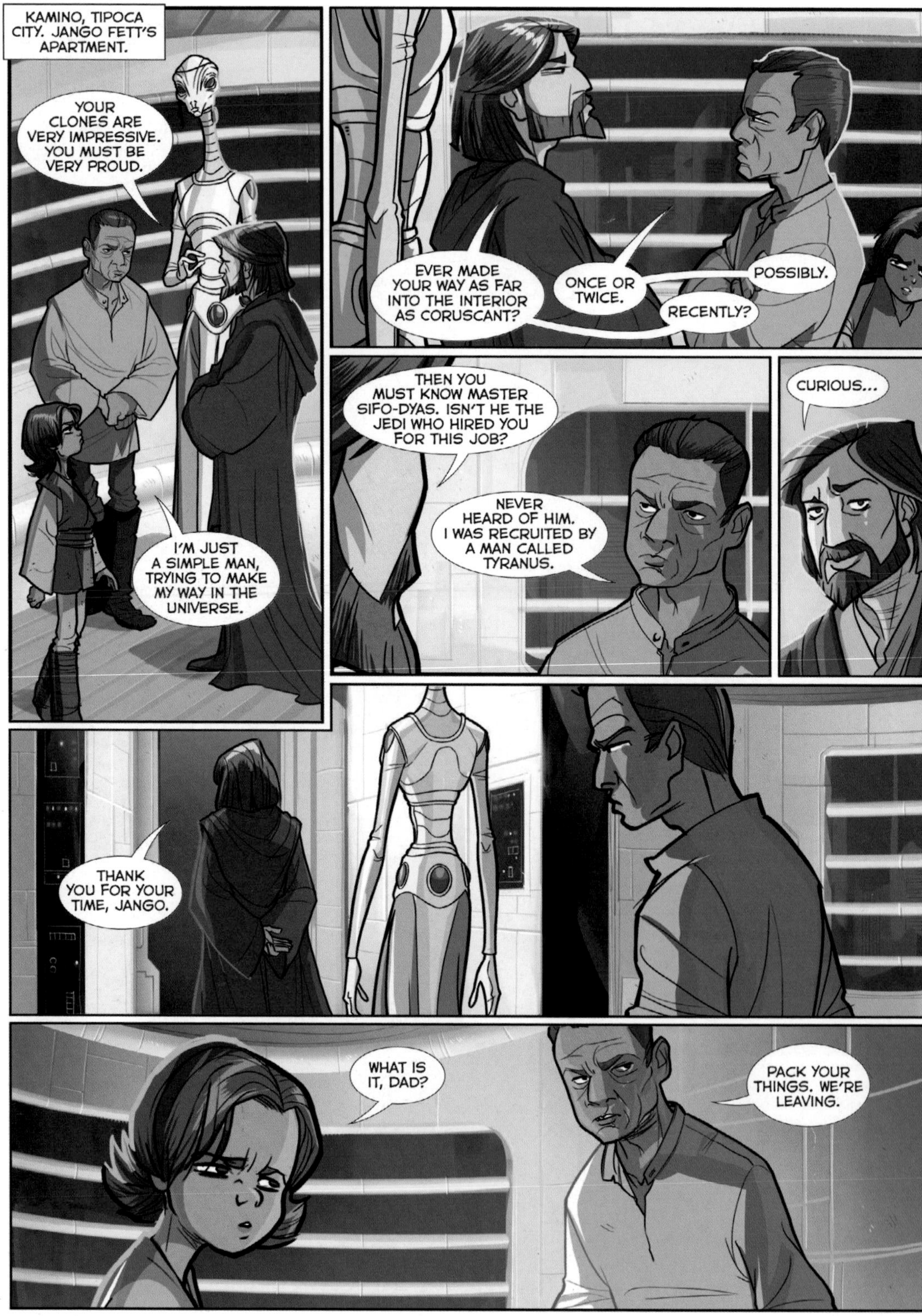
KAMINO, TIPOCA CITY. JANGO FETT'S APARTMENT.
YOUR CLONES ARE VERY IMPRESSIVE. YOU MUST BE VERY PROUD.
I'M JUST A SIMPLE MAN, TRYING TO MAKE MY WAY IN THE UNIVERSE.
EVER MADE YOUR WAY AS FAR INTO THE INTERIOR AS CORUSCANT?
ONCE OR TWICE.
POSSIBLY.
RECENTLY?
THEN YOU MUST KNOW MASTER SIFO-DYAS. ISN'T HE THE JEDI WHO HIRED YOU FOR THIS JOB?
NEVER HEARD OF HIM. I WAS RECRUITED BY A MAN CALLED TYRANUS.
CURIOUS...
THANK YOU FOR YOUR TIME, JANGO.
WHAT IS IT, DAD?
PACK YOUR THINGS. WE'RE LEAVING.

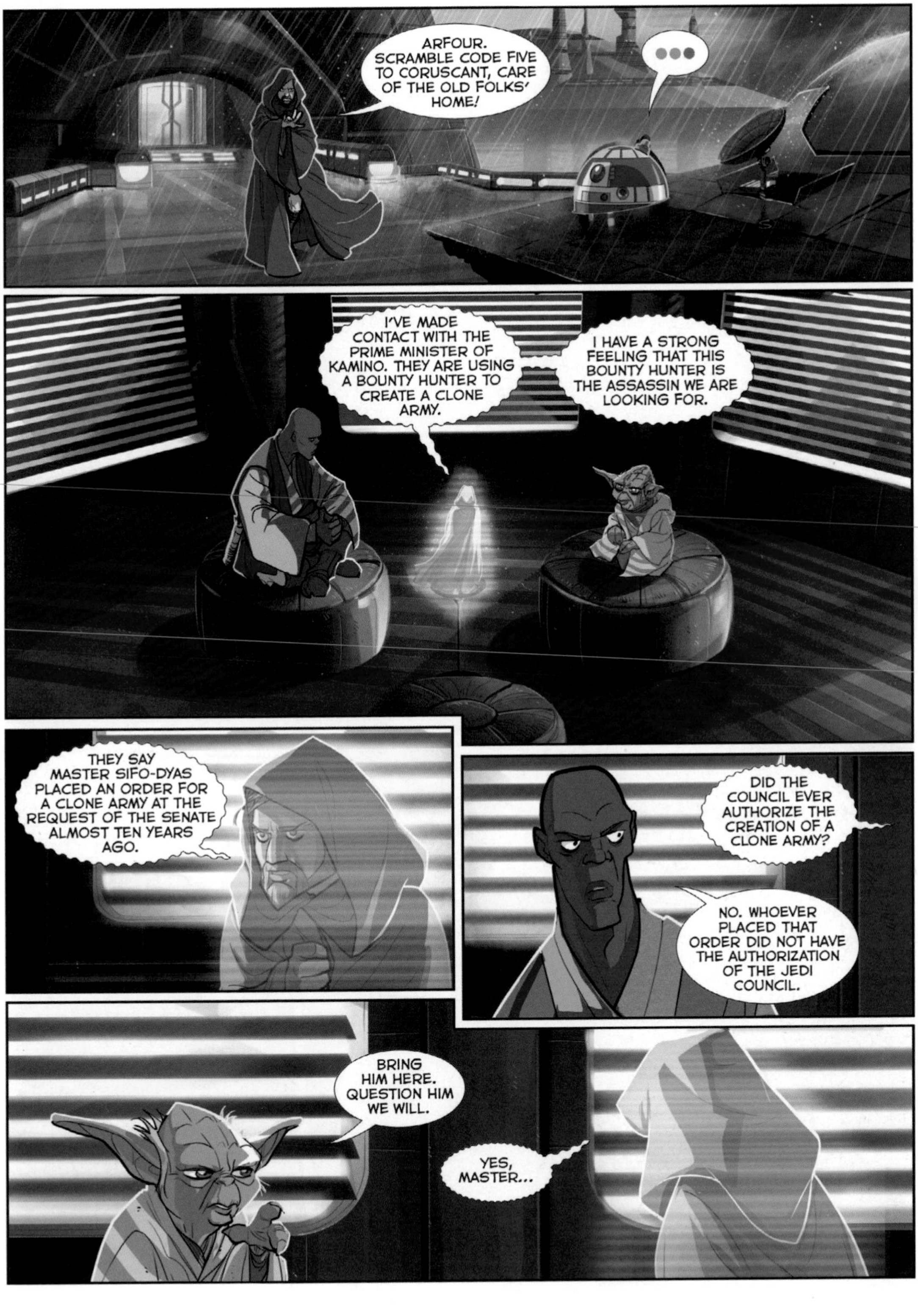
ARFOUR. SCRAMBLE CODE FIVE TO CORUSCANT, CARE OF THE OLD FOLKS' HOME!
•••
I'VE MADE CONTACT WITH THE PRIME MINISTER OF KAMINO. THEY ARE USING A BOUNTY HUNTER TO CREATE A CLONE ARMY.
I HAVE A STRONG FEELING THAT THIS BOUNTY HUNTER IS THE ASSASSIN WE ARE LOOKING FOR.
THEY SAY MASTER SIFO-DYAS PLACED AN ORDER FOR A CLONE ARMY AT THE REQUEST OF THE SENATE ALMOST TEN YEARS AGO.
DID THE COUNCIL EVER AUTHORIZE THE CREATION OF A CLONE ARMY?
NO. WHOEVER PLACED THAT ORDER DID NOT HAVE THE AUTHORIZATION OF THE JEDI COUNCIL.
BRING HIM HERE. QUESTION HIM WE WILL.
YES, MASTER...

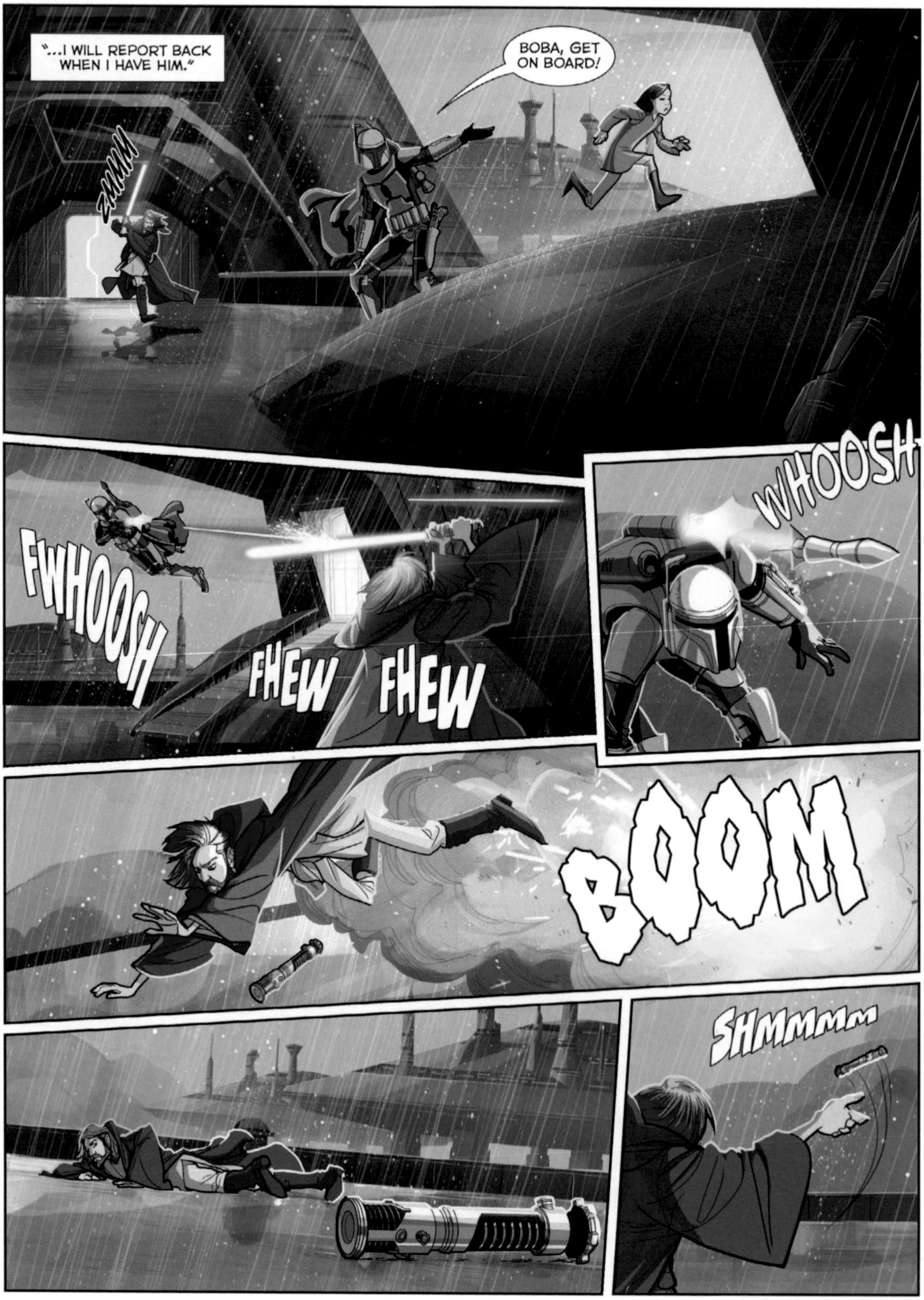
"...I WILL REPORT BACK WHEN I HAVE HIM."
BOBA, GET ON BOARD!
ZHMM
FWHOOSH
FHEW FHEW
WHOOSH
BOOM
SHMMMM

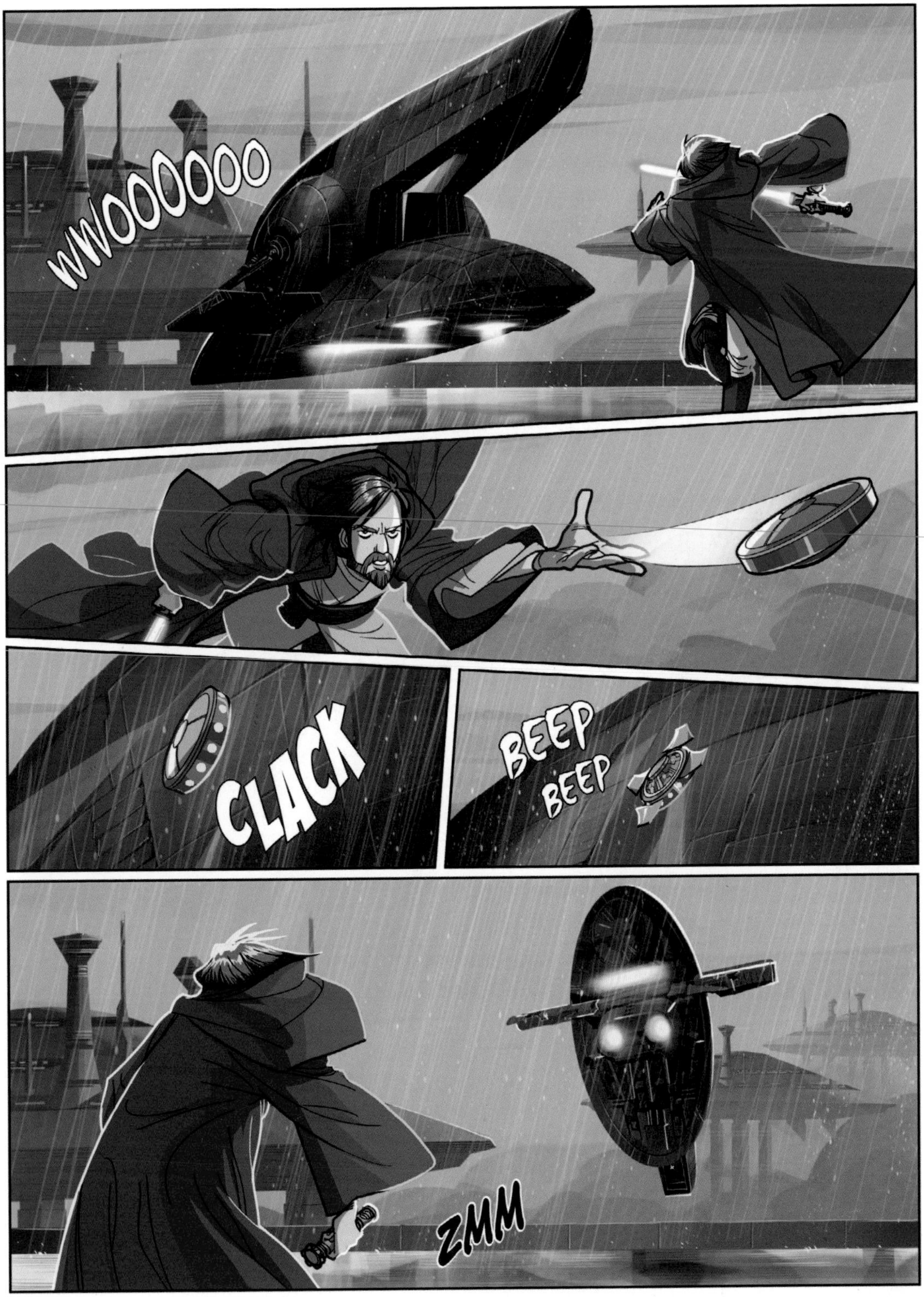
WWOOOOOO
CLACK
BEEP
BEEP
ZMM

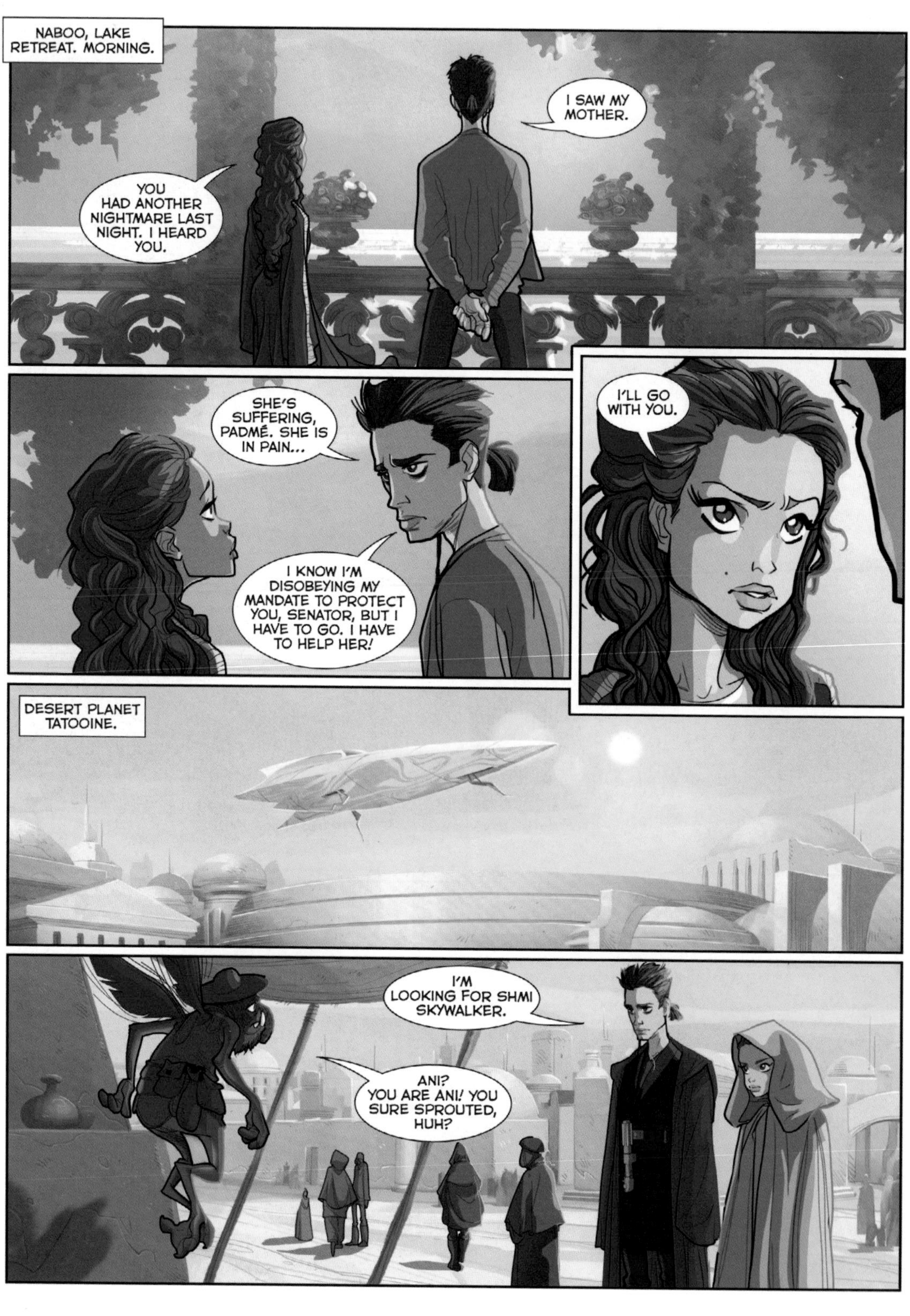
NABOO, LAKE RETREAT. MORNING.
YOU HAD ANOTHER NIGHTMARE LAST NIGHT. I HEARD YOU.
I SAW MY MOTHER.
SHE'S SUFFERING, PADMÉ. SHE IS IN PAIN...
I KNOW I'M DISOBEYING MY MANDATE TO PROTECT YOU, SENATOR, BUT I HAVE TO GO. I HAVE TO HELP HER!
I'LL GO WITH YOU.
DESERT PLANET TATOOINE.
I'M LOOKING FOR SHMI SKYWALKER.
ANI? YOU ARE ANI! YOU SURE SPROUTED, HUH?

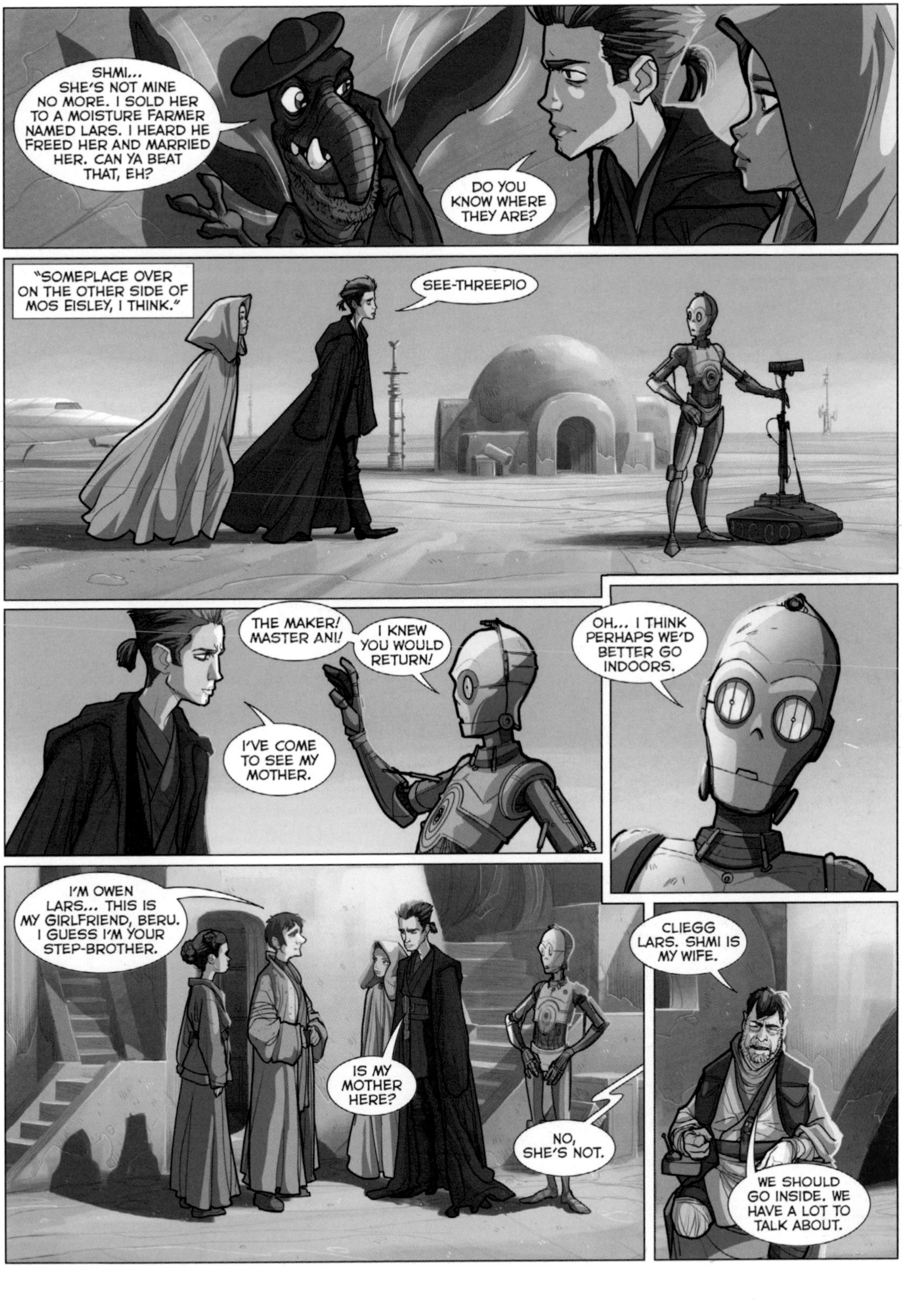
SHMI... SHE'S NOT MINE NO MORE. I SOLD HER TO A MOISTURE FARMER NAMED LARS. I HEARD HE FREED HER AND MARRIED HER. CAN YA BEAT THAT, EH?
DO YOU KNOW WHERE THEY ARE?
"SOMEPLACE OVER ON THE OTHER SIDE OF MOS EISLEY, I THINK."
SEE-THREEPIO
THE MAKER! MASTER ANI!
I KNEW YOU WOULD RETURN!
I'VE COME TO SEE MY MOTHER.
OH... I THINK PERHAPS WE'D BETTER GO INDOORS.
I'M OWEN LARS... THIS IS MY GIRLFRIEND, BERU. I GUESS I'M YOUR STEP-BROTHER.
IS MY MOTHER HERE?
NO, SHE'S NOT.
CLIEGG LARS. SHMI IS MY WIFE.
WE SHOULD GO INSIDE. WE HAVE A LOT TO TALK ABOUT.

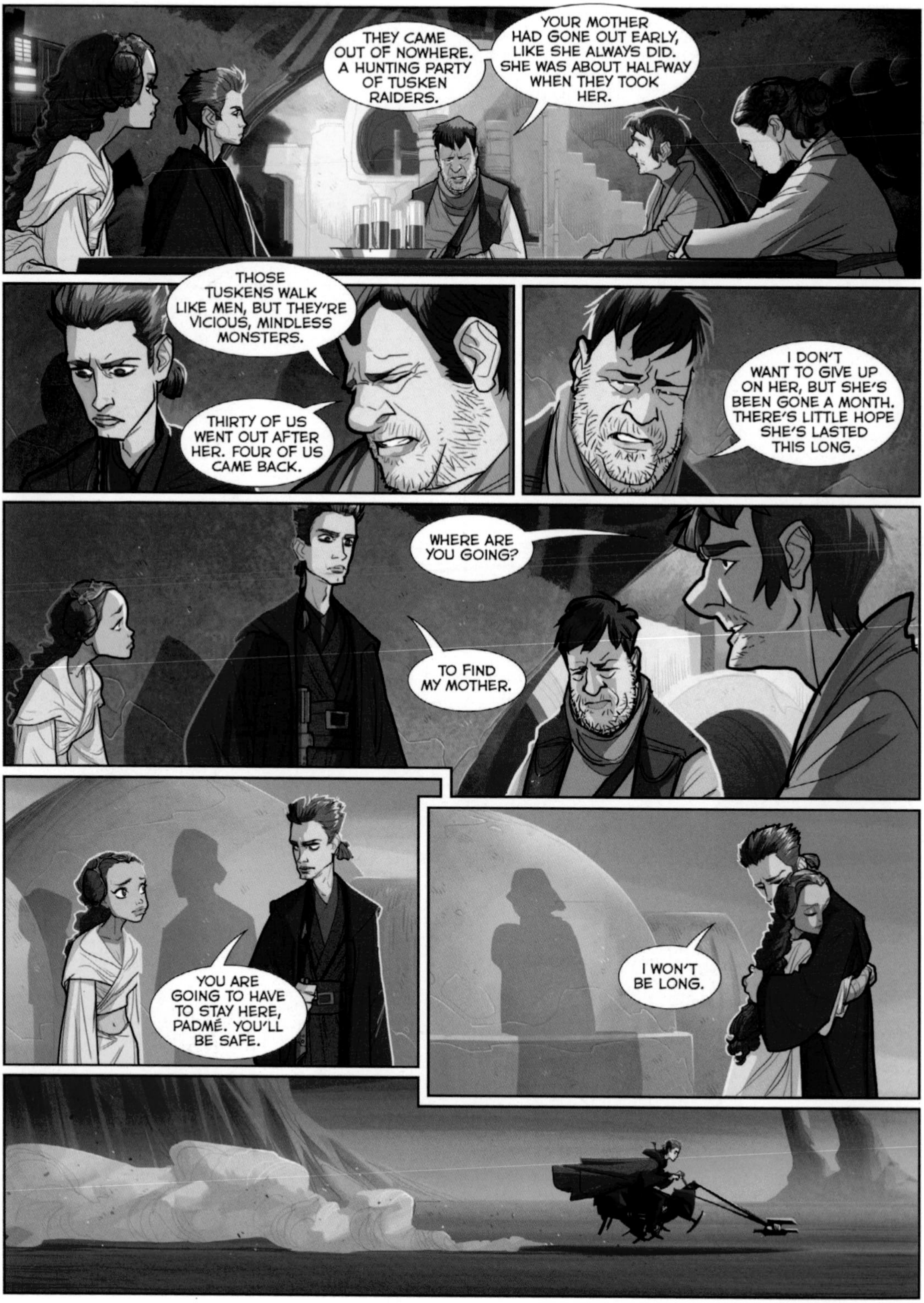
THEY CAME OUT OF NOWHERE. A HUNTING PARTY OF TUSKEN RAIDERS.
YOUR MOTHER HAD GONE OUT EARLY, LIKE SHE ALWAYS DID. SHE WAS ABOUT HALFWAY WHEN THEY TOOK HER.
THOSE TUSKENS WALK LIKE MEN, BUT THEY'RE VICIOUS, MINDLESS MONSTERS.
THIRTY OF US WENT OUT AFTER HER. FOUR OF US CAME BACK.
I DON'T WANT TO GIVE UP ON HER, BUT SHE'S BEEN GONE A MONTH. THERE'S LITTLE HOPE SHE'S LASTED THIS LONG.
WHERE ARE YOU GOING?
TO FIND MY MOTHER.
YOU ARE GOING TO HAVE TO STAY HERE, PADMÉ. YOU'LL BE SAFE.
I WON'T BE LONG.

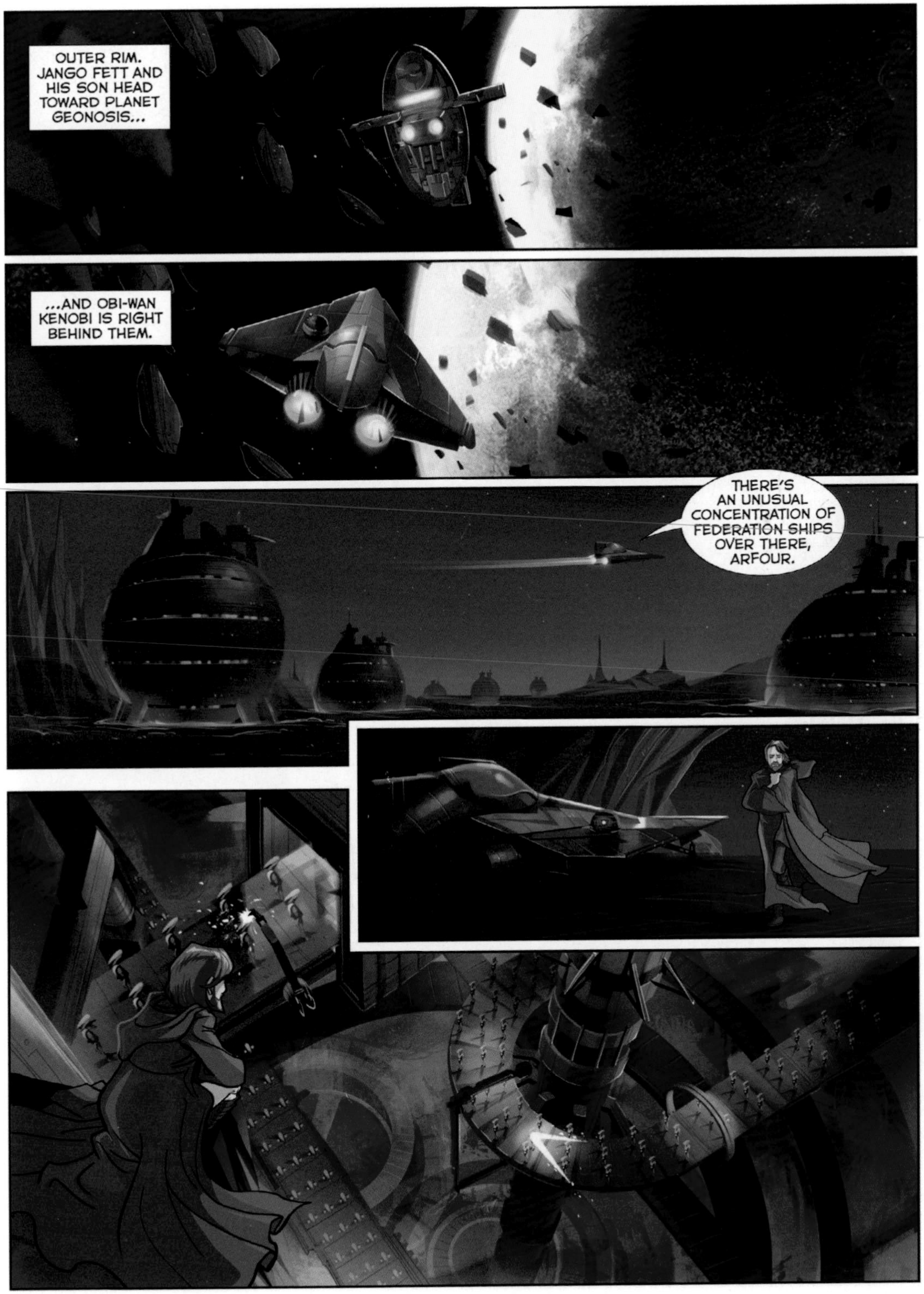

OUTER RIM. JANGO FETT AND HIS SON HEAD TOWARD PLANET GEONOSIS...
...AND OBI-WAN KENOBI IS RIGHT BEHIND THEM.
THERE'S AN UNUSUAL CONCENTRATION OF FEDERATION SHIPS OVER THERE, ARFOUR.

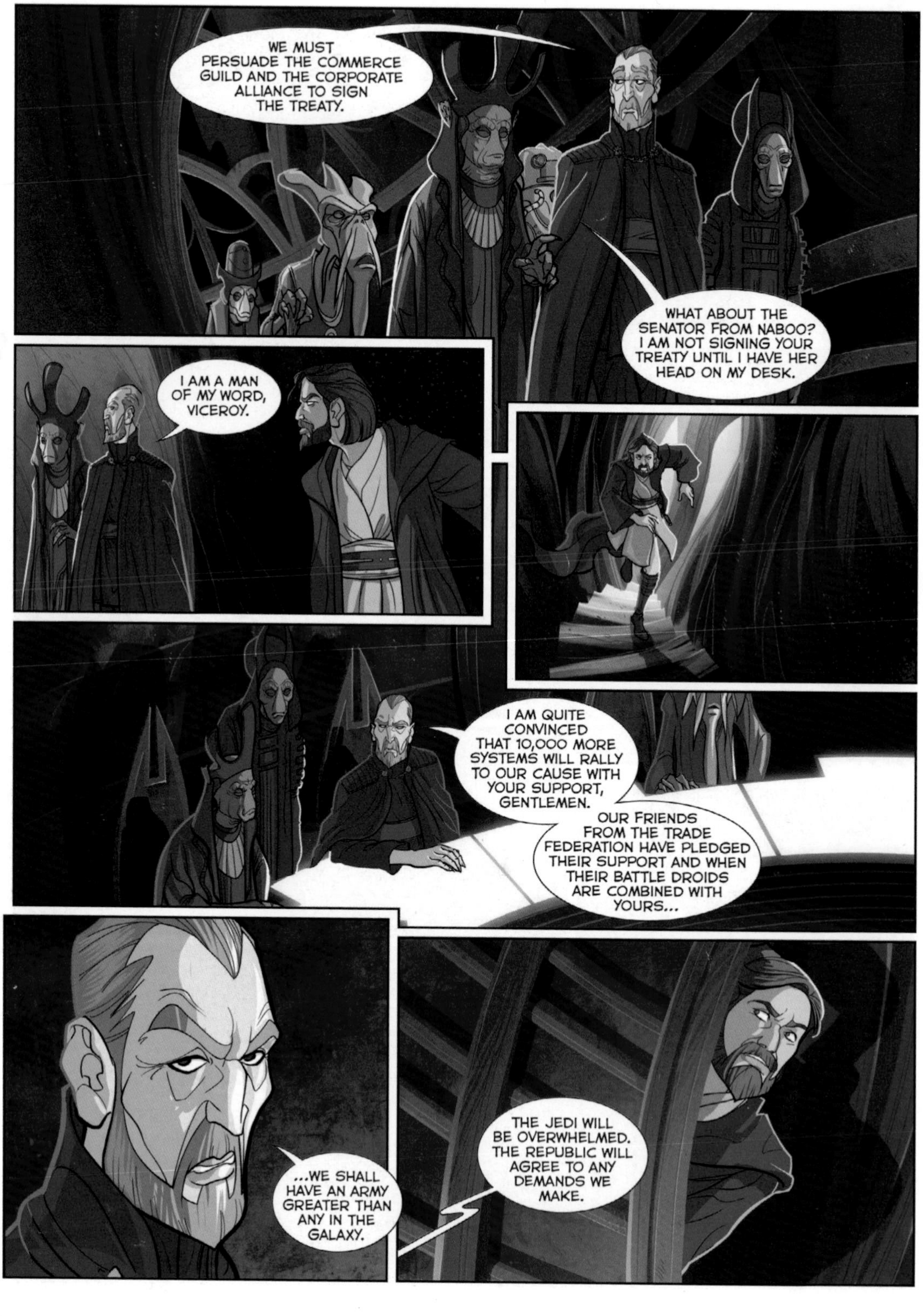
WE MUST PERSUADE THE COMMERCE GUILD AND THE CORPORATE ALLIANCE TO SIGN THE TREATY.
WHAT ABOUT THE SENATOR FROM NABOO? I AM NOT SIGNING YOUR TREATY UNTIL I HAVE HER HEAD ON MY DESK.
I AM A MAN OF MY WORD, VICEROY.
I AM QUITE CONVINCED THAT 10,000 MORE SYSTEMS WILL RALLY TO OUR CAUSE WITH YOUR SUPPORT, GENTLEMEN.
OUR FRIENDS FROM THE TRADE FEDERATION HAVE PLEDGED THEIR SUPPORT AND WHEN THEIR BATTLE DROIDS ARE COMBINED WITH YOURS...
...WE SHALL HAVE AN ARMY GREATER THAN ANY IN THE GALAXY.
THE JEDI WILL BE OVERWHELMED. THE REPUBLIC WILL AGREE TO ANY DEMANDS WE MAKE.

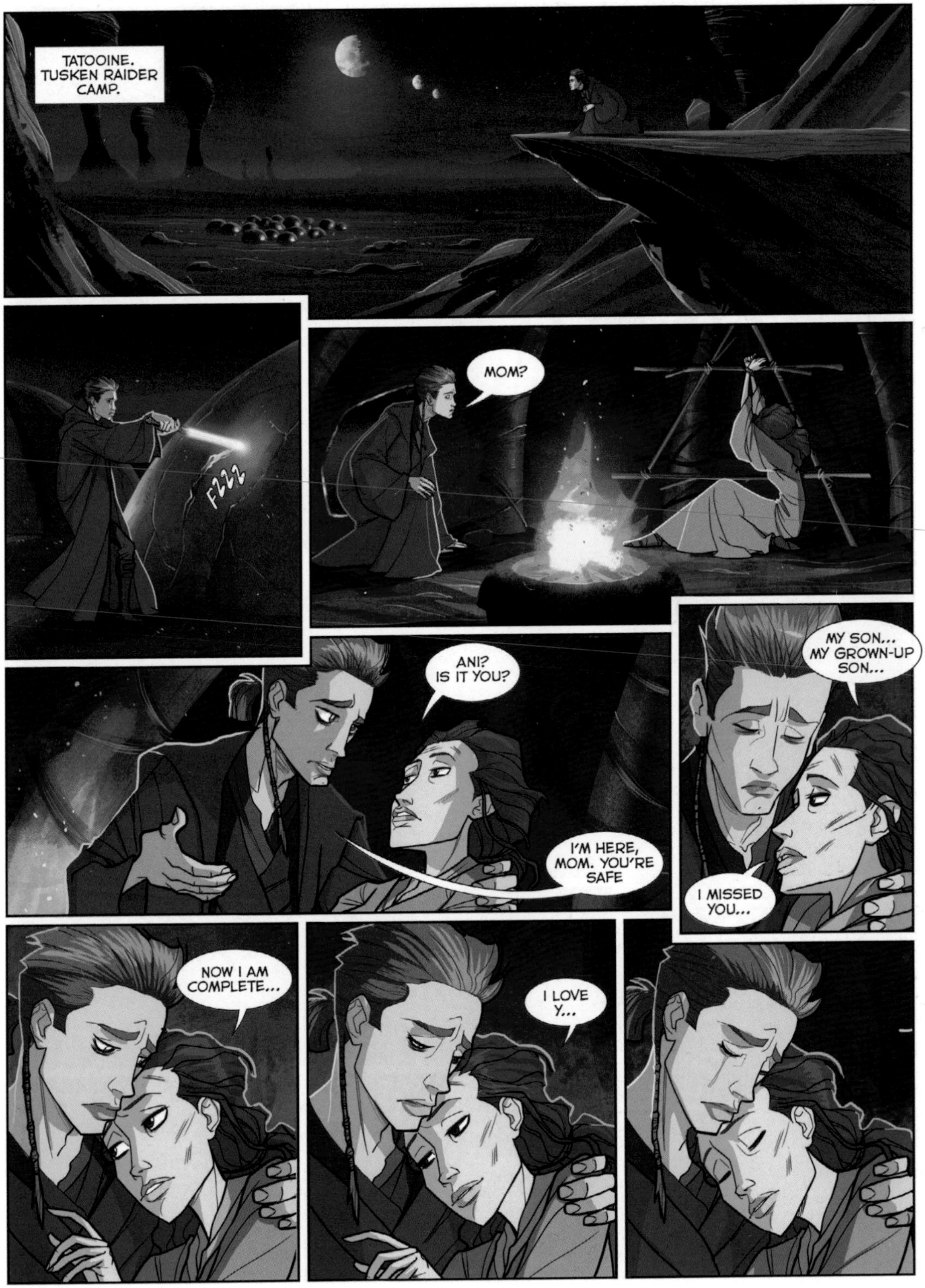

TATOOINE. TUSKEN RAIDER CAMP.
FZZZ
MOM?
ANI? IS IT YOU?
I'M HERE, MOM. YOU'RE SAFE
MY SON... MY GROWN-UP SON...
I MISSED YOU...
NOW I AM COMPLETE...
I LOVE Y...

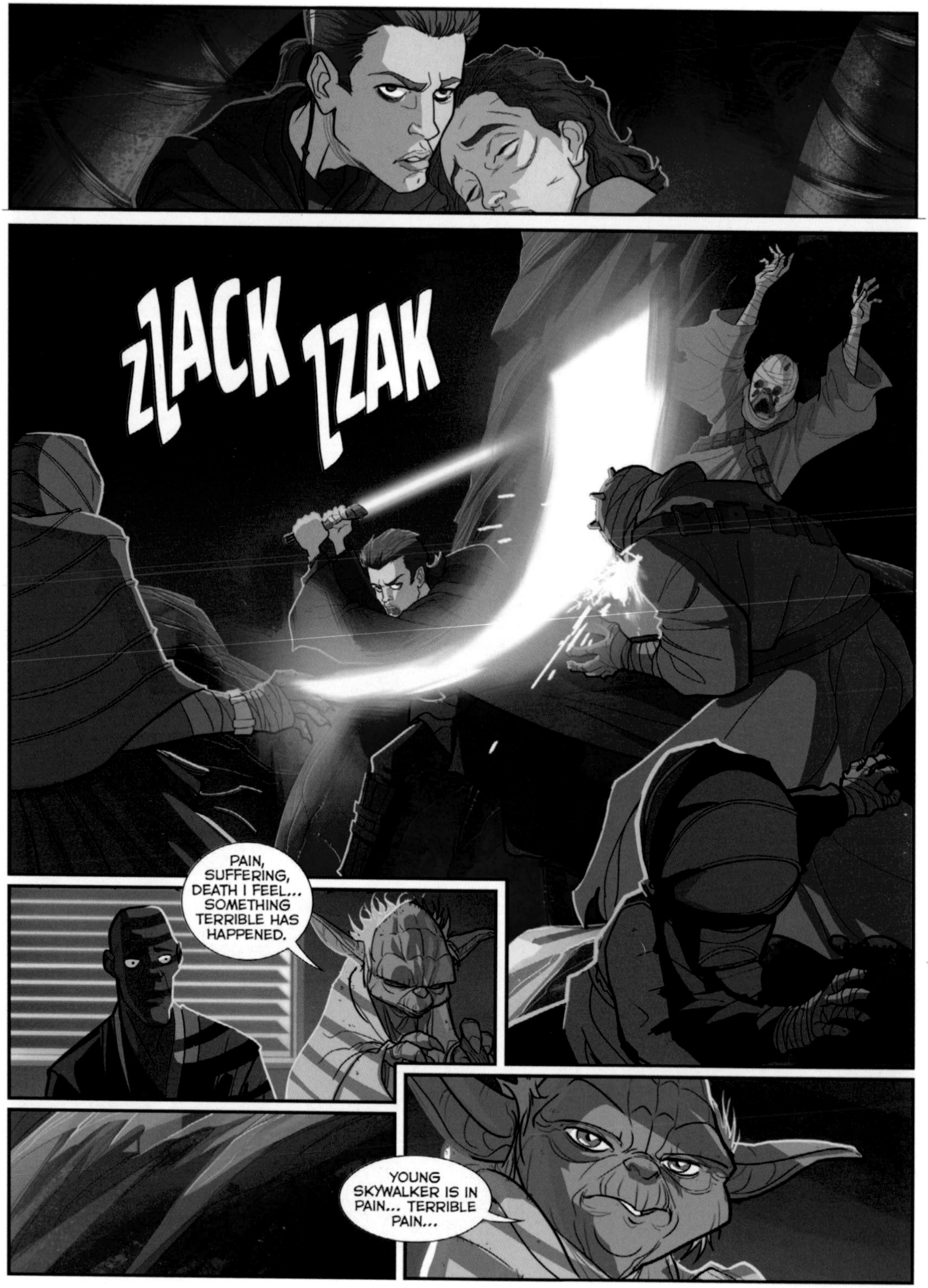
ZZACK ZZAK
PAIN, SUFFERING, DEATH I FEEL... SOMETHING TERRIBLE HAS HAPPENED.
YOUNG SKYWALKER IS IN PAIN... TERRIBLE PAIN...

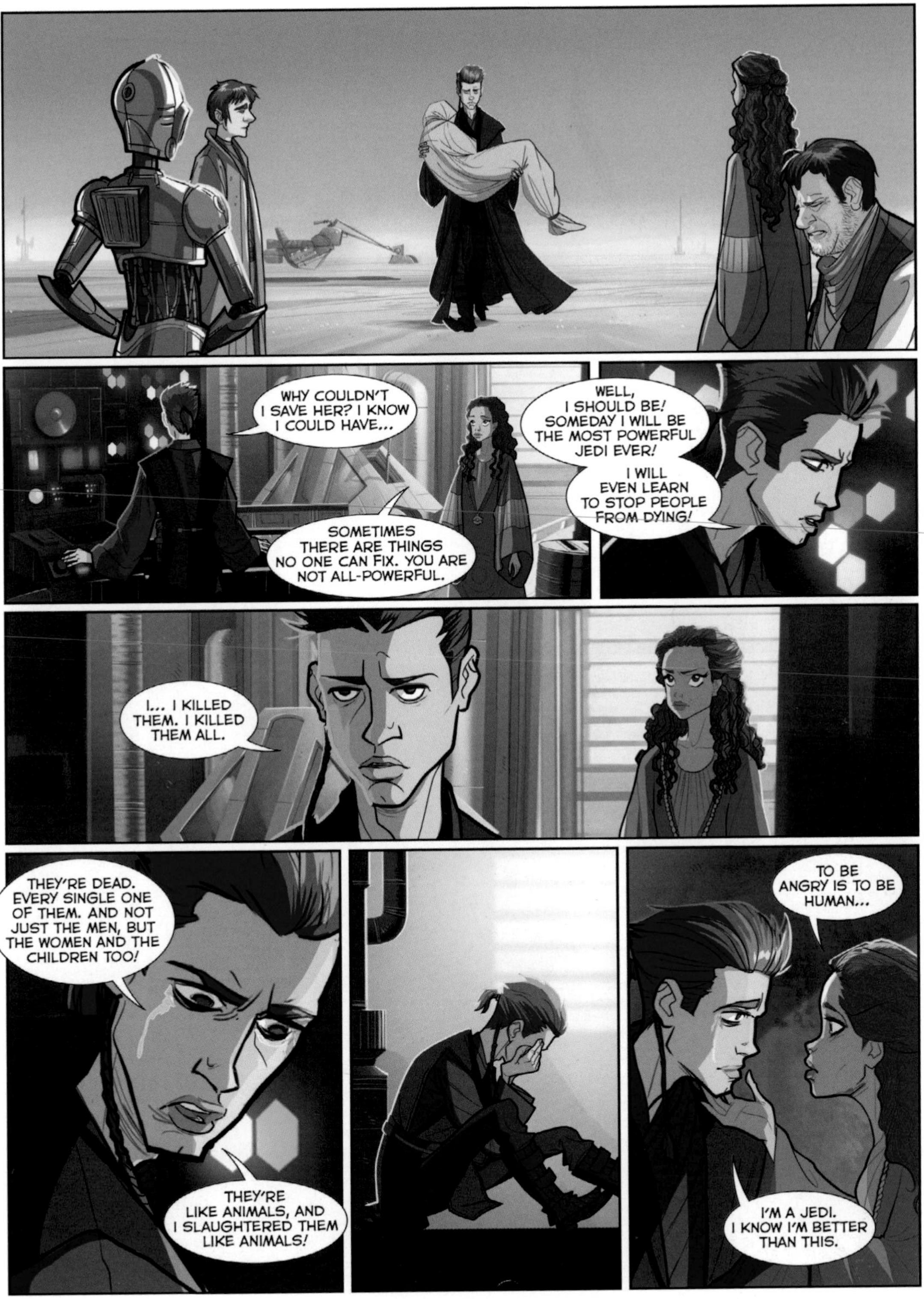
WHY COULDN'T I SAVE HER? I KNOW I COULD HAVE...
SOMETIMES THERE ARE THINGS NO ONE CAN FIX. YOU ARE NOT ALL-POWERFUL.
WELL, I SHOULD BE! SOMEDAY I WILL BE THE MOST POWERFUL JEDI EVER!
I WILL EVEN LEARN TO STOP PEOPLE FROM DYING!
I... I KILLED THEM. I KILLED THEM ALL.
THEY'RE DEAD. EVERY SINGLE ONE OF THEM. AND NOT JUST THE MEN, BUT THE WOMEN AND THE CHILDREN TOO!
THEY'RE LIKE ANIMALS, AND I SLAUGHTERED THEM LIKE ANIMALS!
TO BE ANGRY IS TO BE HUMAN...
I'M A JEDI. I KNOW I'M BETTER THAN THIS.

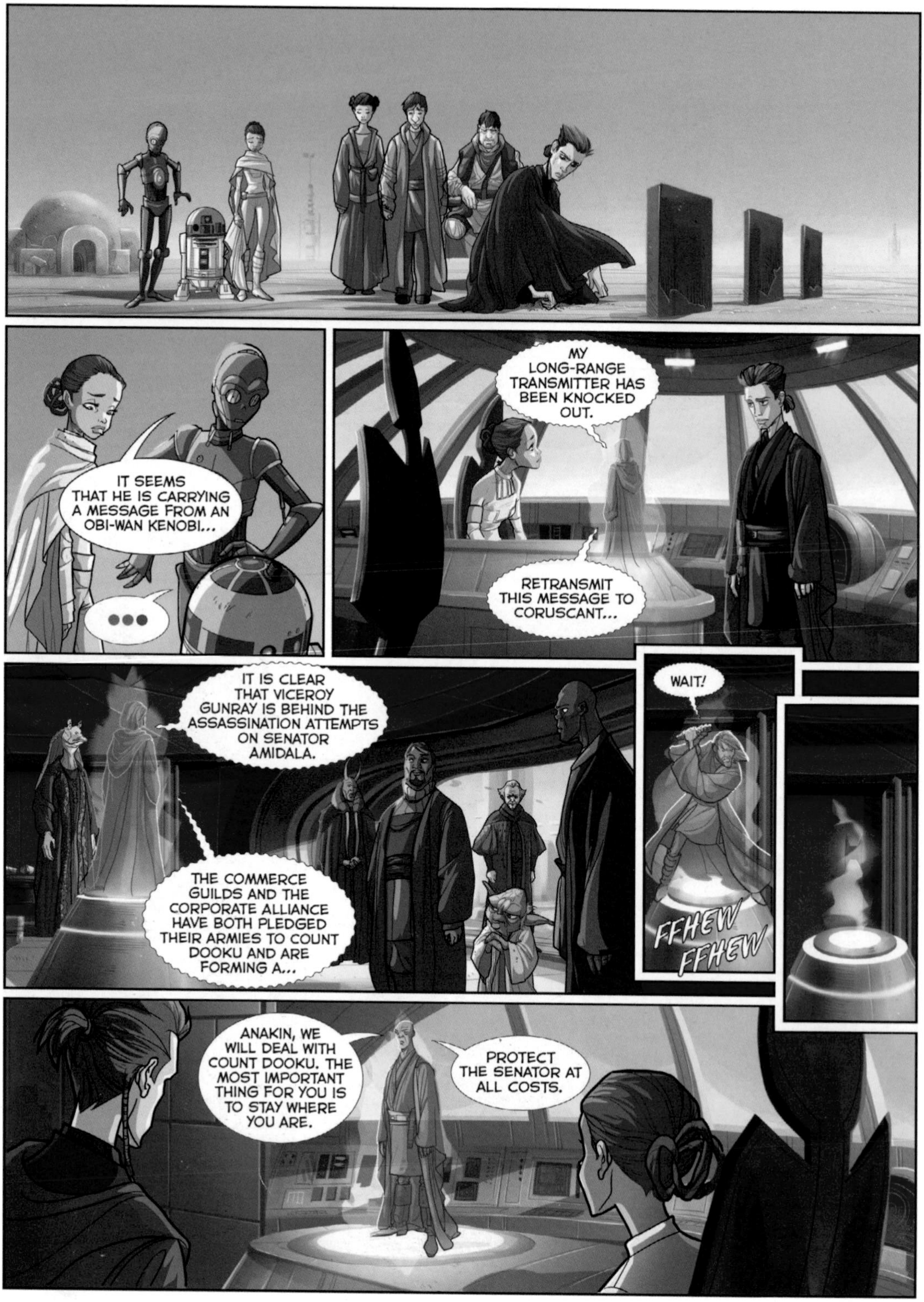

IT SEEMS THAT HE IS CARRYING A MESSAGE FROM AN OBI-WAN KENOBI...
•••
MY LONG-RANGE TRANSMITTER HAS BEEN KNOCKED OUT.
RETRANSMIT THIS MESSAGE TO CORUSCANT...
IT IS CLEAR THAT VICEROY GUNRAY IS BEHIND THE ASSASSINATION ATTEMPTS ON SENATOR AMIDALA.
THE COMMERCE GUILDS AND THE CORPORATE ALLIANCE HAVE BOTH PLEDGED THEIR ARMIES TO COUNT DOOKU AND ARE FORMING A...
WAIT!
FFHEW FFHEW
ANAKIN, WE WILL DEAL WITH COUNT DOOKU. THE MOST IMPORTANT THING FOR YOU IS TO STAY WHERE YOU ARE.
PROTECT THE SENATOR AT ALL COSTS.

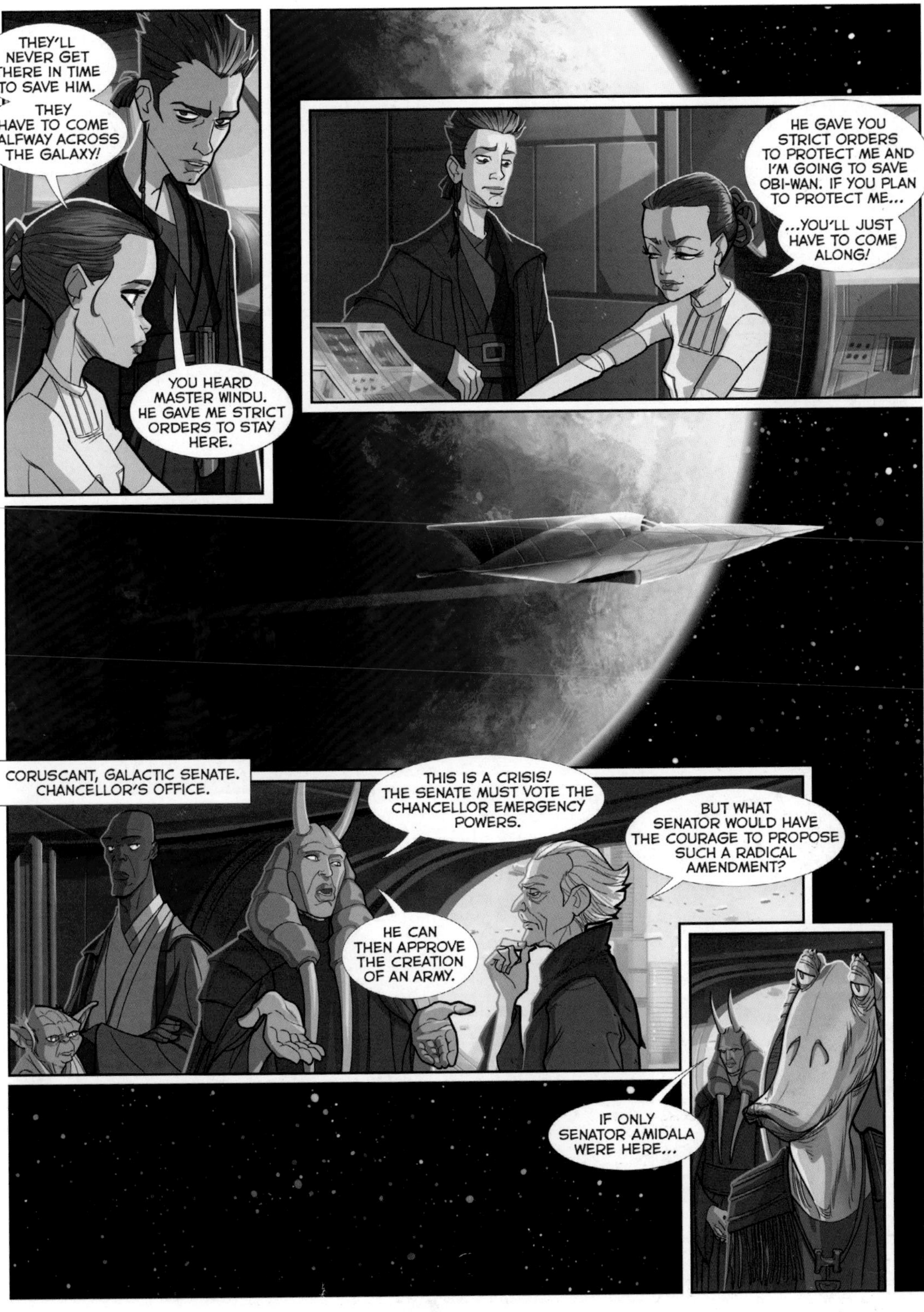
THEY'LL NEVER GET THERE IN TIME TO SAVE HIM.
THEY HAVE TO COME HALFWAY ACROSS THE GALAXY!
YOU HEARD MASTER WINDU. HE GAVE ME STRICT ORDERS TO STAY HERE.
HE GAVE YOU STRICT ORDERS TO PROTECT ME AND I'M GOING TO SAVE OBI-WAN. IF YOU PLAN TO PROTECT ME...
...YOU'LL JUST HAVE TO COME ALONG!
CORUSCANT, GALACTIC SENATE. CHANCELLOR'S OFFICE.
THIS IS A CRISIS! THE SENATE MUST VOTE THE CHANCELLOR EMERGENCY POWERS.
HE CAN THEN APPROVE THE CREATION OF AN ARMY.
BUT WHAT SENATOR WOULD HAVE THE COURAGE TO PROPOSE SUCH A RADICAL AMENDMENT?
IF ONLY SENATOR AMIDALA WERE HERE...

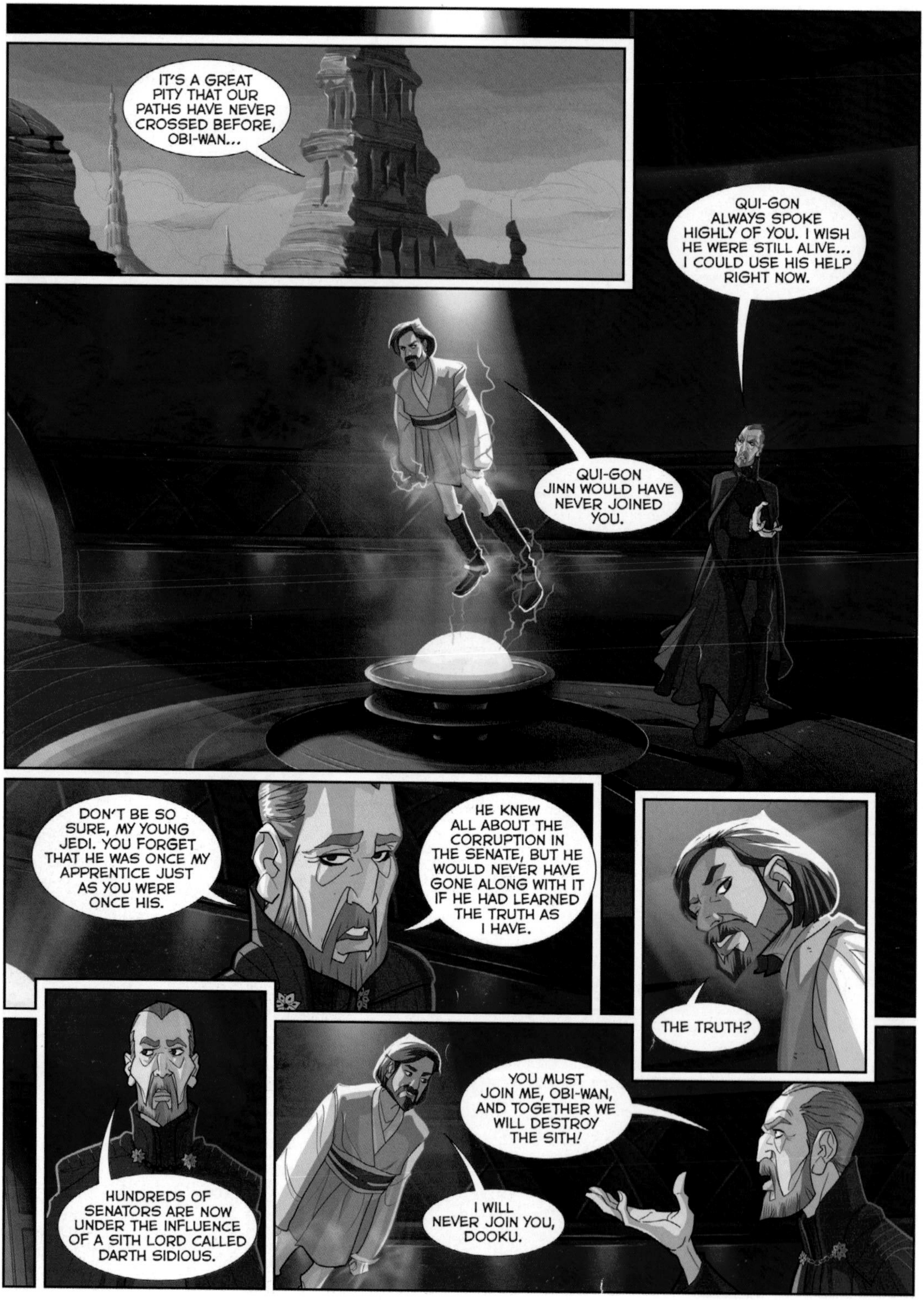
IT'S A GREAT PITY THAT OUR PATHS HAVE NEVER CROSSED BEFORE, OBI-WAN...
QUI-GON ALWAYS SPOKE HIGHLY OF YOU. I WISH HE WERE STILL ALIVE... I COULD USE HIS HELP RIGHT NOW.
QUI-GON JINN WOULD HAVE NEVER JOINED YOU.
DON'T BE SO SURE, MY YOUNG JEDI. YOU FORGET THAT HE WAS ONCE MY APPRENTICE JUST AS YOU WERE ONCE HIS.
HE KNEW ALL ABOUT THE CORRUPTION IN THE SENATE, BUT HE WOULD NEVER HAVE GONE ALONG WITH IT IF HE HAD LEARNED THE TRUTH AS I HAVE.
THE TRUTH?
HUNDREDS OF SENATORS ARE NOW UNDER THE INFLUENCE OF A SITH LORD CALLED DARTH SIDIOUS.
YOU MUST JOIN ME, OBI-WAN, AND TOGETHER WE WILL DESTROY THE SITH!
I WILL NEVER JOIN YOU, DOOKU.

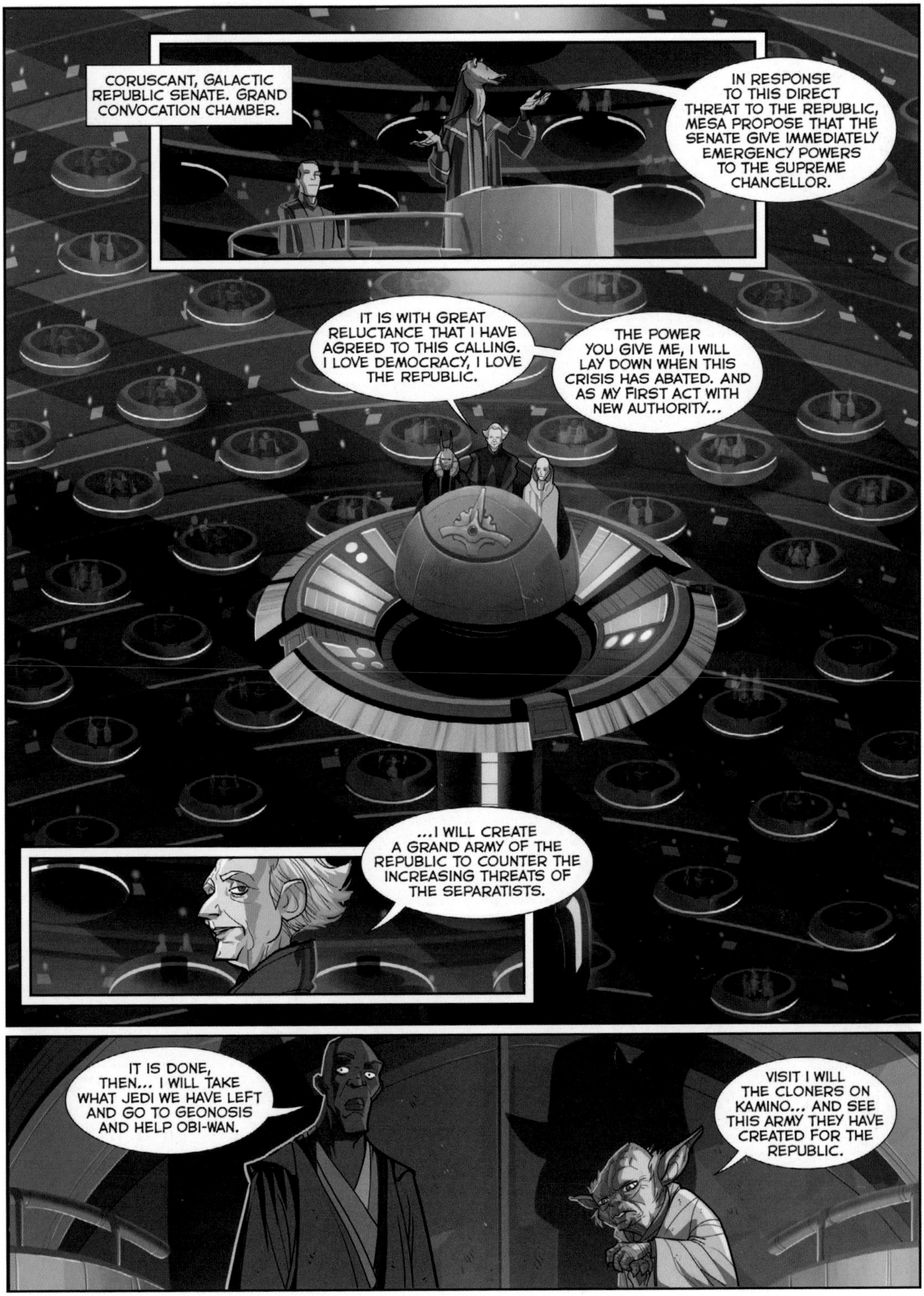
CORUSCANT, GALACTIC REPUBLIC SENATE. GRAND CONVOCATION CHAMBER.
IN RESPONSE TO THIS DIRECT THREAT TO THE REPUBLIC, MESA PROPOSE THAT THE SENATE GIVE IMMEDIATELY EMERGENCY POWERS TO THE SUPREME CHANCELLOR.
IT IS WITH GREAT RELUCTANCE THAT I HAVE AGREED TO THIS CALLING. I LOVE DEMOCRACY, I LOVE THE REPUBLIC.
THE POWER YOU GIVE ME, I WILL LAY DOWN WHEN THIS CRISIS HAS ABATED. AND AS MY FIRST ACT WITH NEW AUTHORITY...
...I WILL CREATE A GRAND ARMY OF THE REPUBLIC TO COUNTER THE INCREASING THREATS OF THE SEPARATISTS.
IT IS DONE, THEN... I WILL TAKE WHAT JEDI WE HAVE LEFT AND GO TO GEONOSIS AND HELP OBI-WAN.
VISIT I WILL THE CLONERS ON KAMINO... AND SEE THIS ARMY THEY HAVE CREATED FOR THE REPUBLIC.

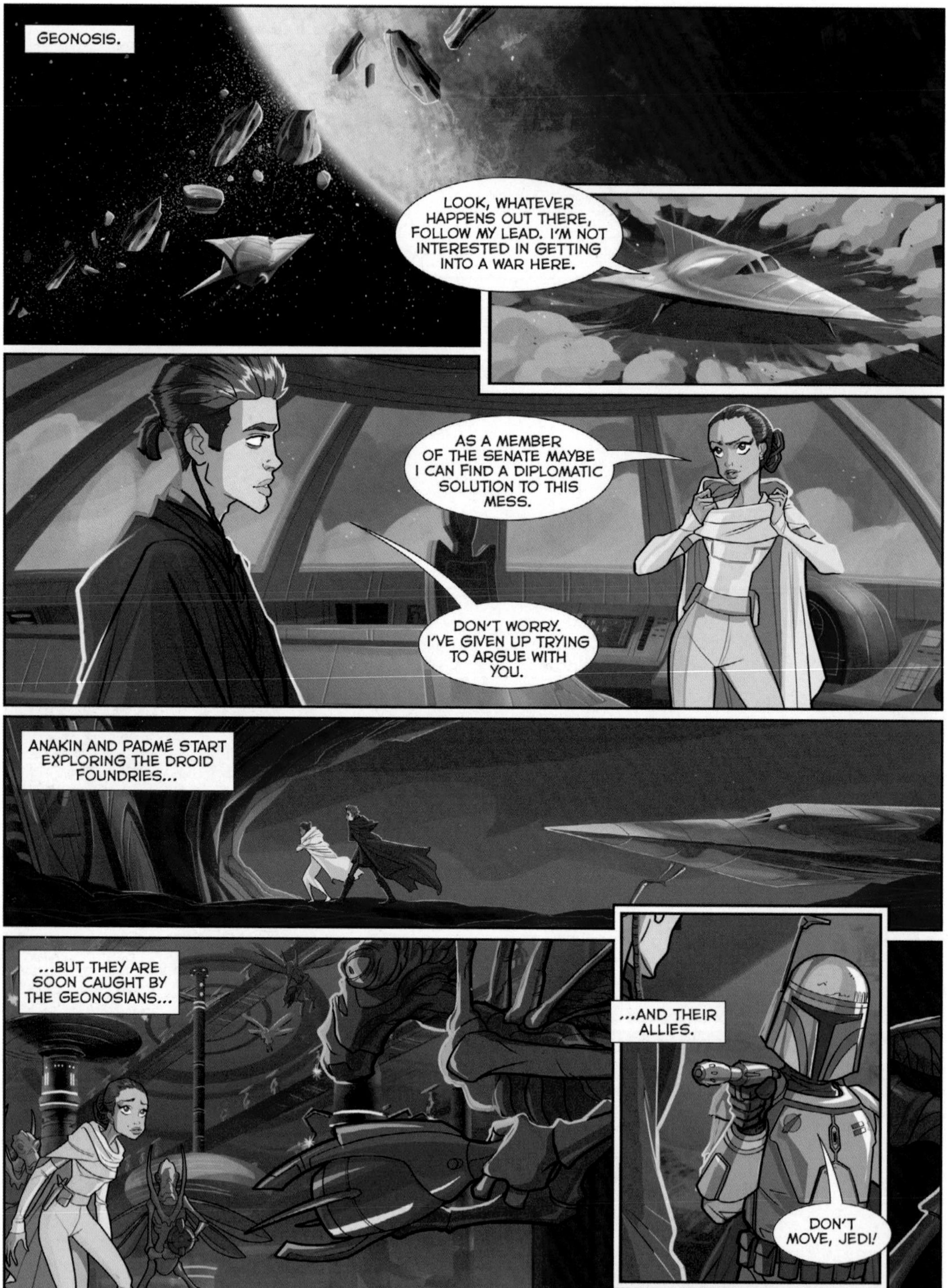
GEONOSIS.
LOOK, WHATEVER HAPPENS OUT THERE, FOLLOW MY LEAD. I'M NOT INTERESTED IN GETTING INTO A WAR HERE.
AS A MEMBER OF THE SENATE MAYBE I CAN FIND A DIPLOMATIC SOLUTION TO THIS MESS.
DON'T WORRY. I'VE GIVEN UP TRYING TO ARGUE WITH YOU.
ANAKIN AND PADMÉ START EXPLORING THE DROID FOUNDRIES...
...BUT THEY ARE SOON CAUGHT BY THE GEONOSIANS...
...AND THEIR ALLIES.
DON'T MOVE, JEDI!

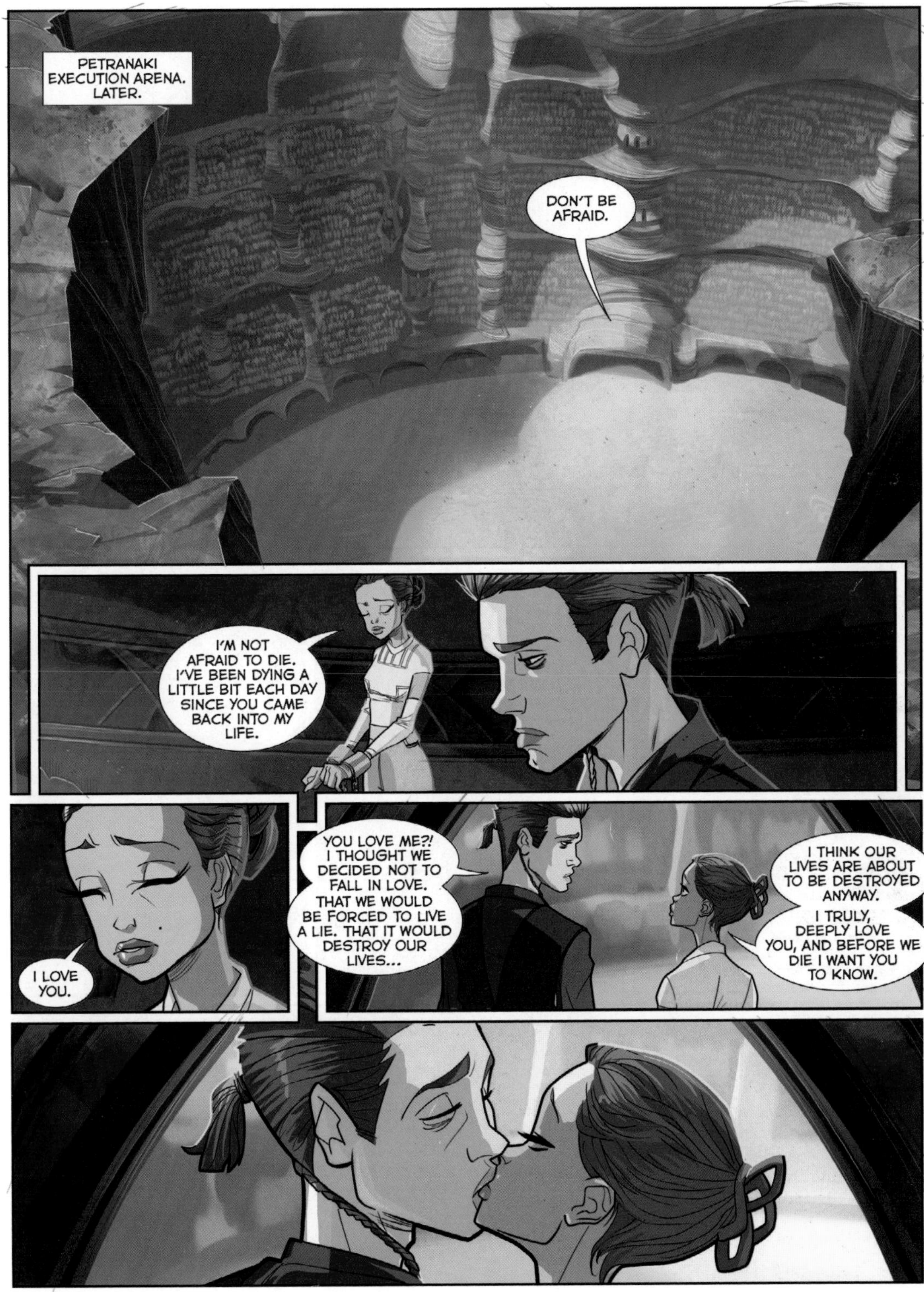
PETRANAKI EXECUTION ARENA. LATER.
DON'T BE AFRAID.
I'M NOT AFRAID TO DIE. I'VE BEEN DYING A LITTLE BIT EACH DAY SINCE YOU CAME BACK INTO MY LIFE.
I LOVE YOU.
YOU LOVE ME?! I THOUGHT WE DECIDED NOT TO FALL IN LOVE. THAT WE WOULD BE FORCED TO LIVE A LIE. THAT IT WOULD DESTROY OUR LIVES...
I THINK OUR LIVES ARE ABOUT TO BE DESTROYED ANYWAY.
I TRULY, DEEPLY LOVE YOU, AND BEFORE WE DIE I WANT YOU TO KNOW.

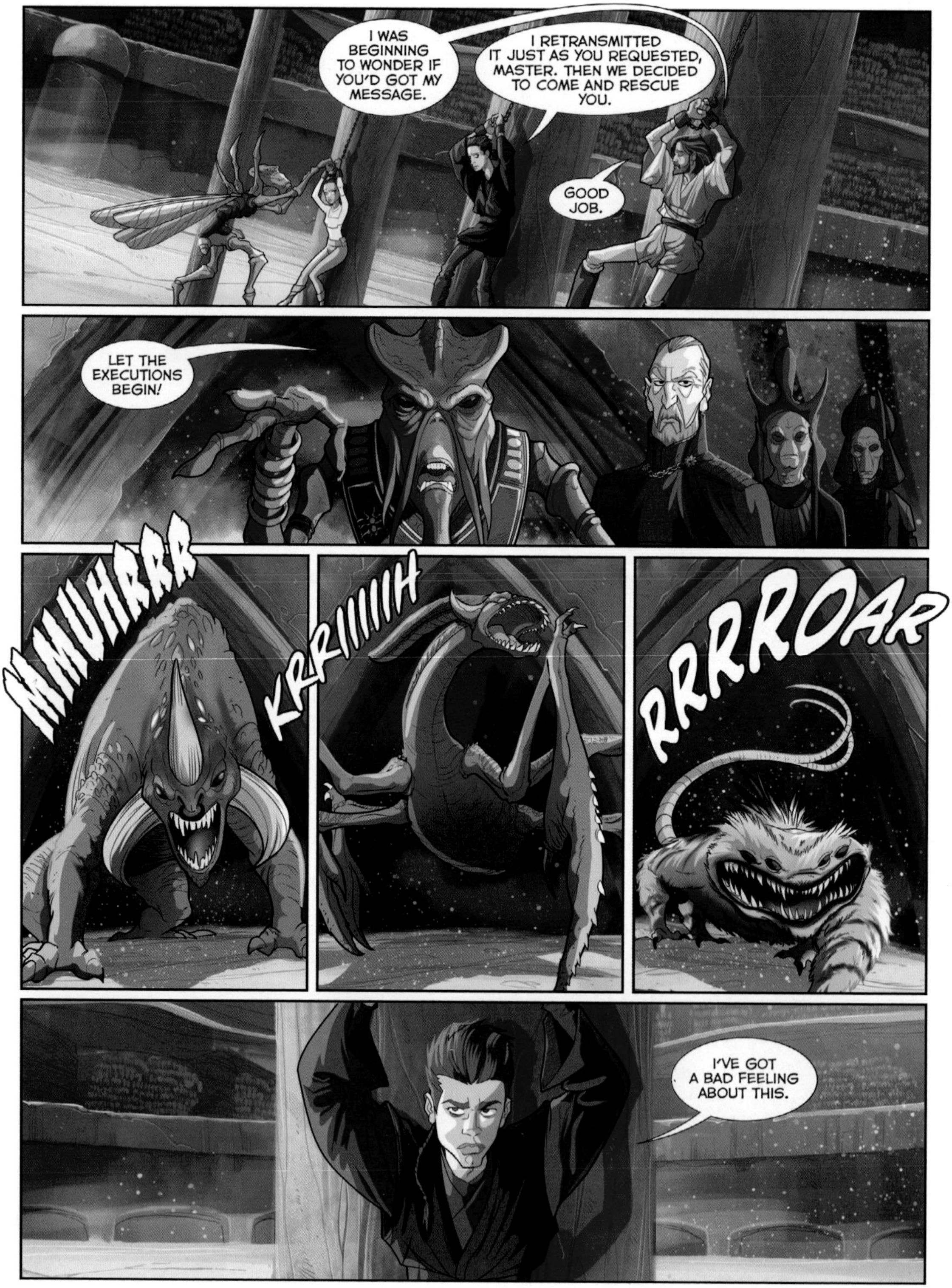
I WAS BEGINNING TO WONDER IF YOU'D GOT MY MESSAGE.
I RETRANSMITTED IT JUST AS YOU REQUESTED, MASTER. THEN WE DECIDED TO COME AND RESCUE YOU.
GOOD JOB.
LET THE EXECUTIONS BEGIN!
MMUHRRR
KRRIIIIIH
RRRROAR
I'VE GOT A BAD FEELING ABOUT THIS.

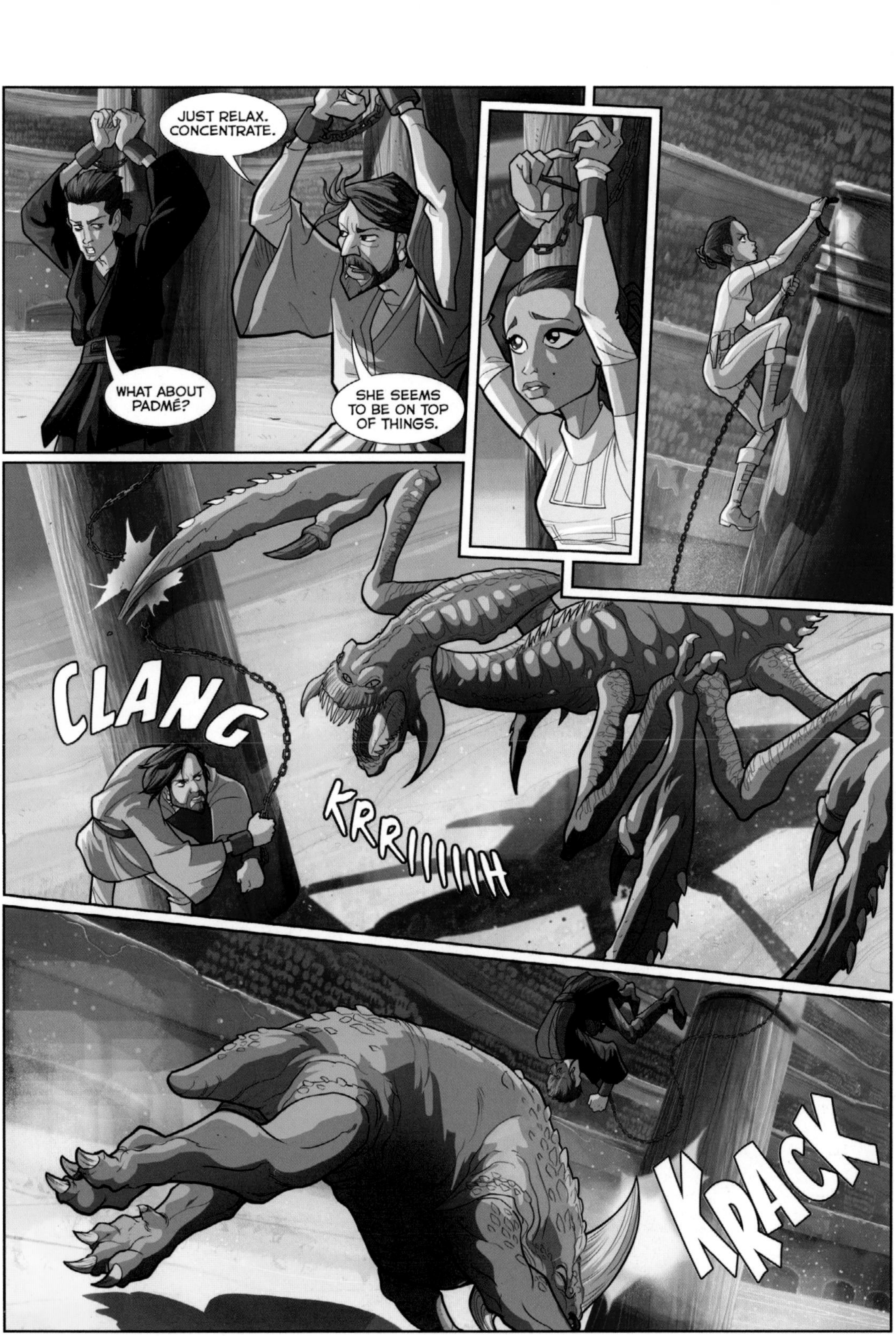
JUST RELAX. CONCENTRATE.
WHAT ABOUT PADMÉ?
SHE SEEMS TO BE ON TOP OF THINGS.
CLANG
KRRIIIIIH
KRACK

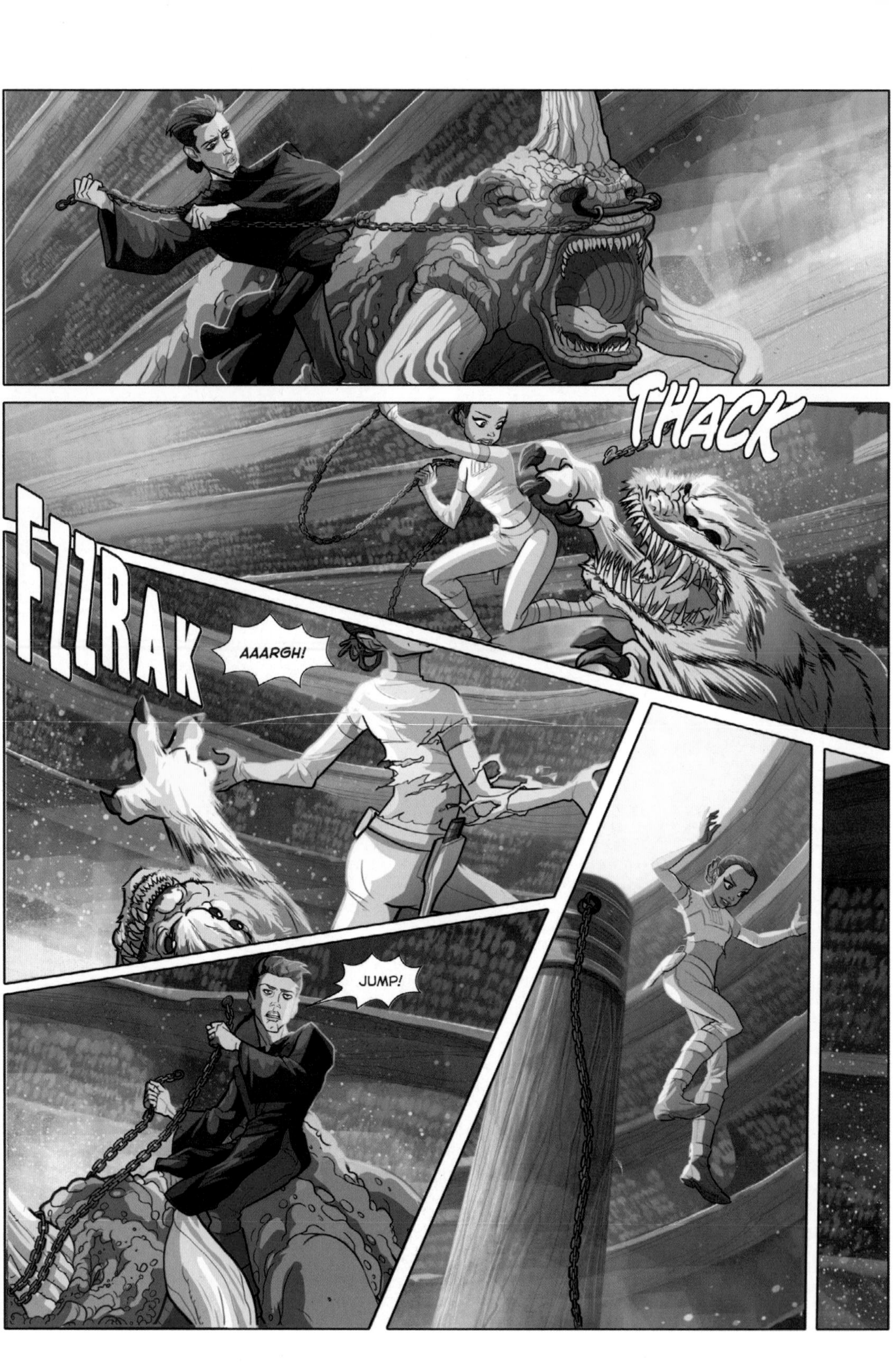
THACK
FZZRAK
AAARGH!
JUMP!

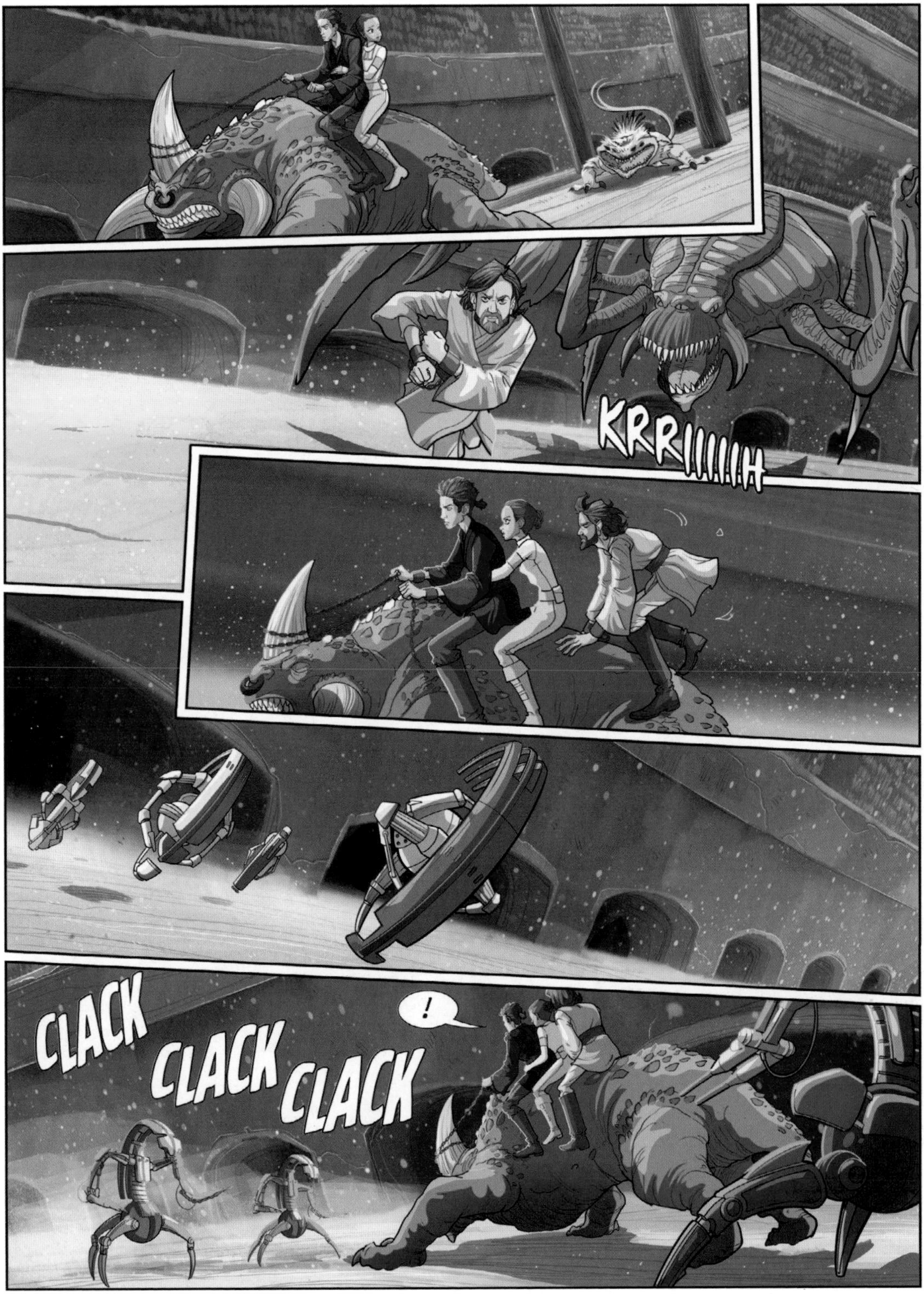
KRRIIIIIIH
!
CLACK
CLACK
CLACK

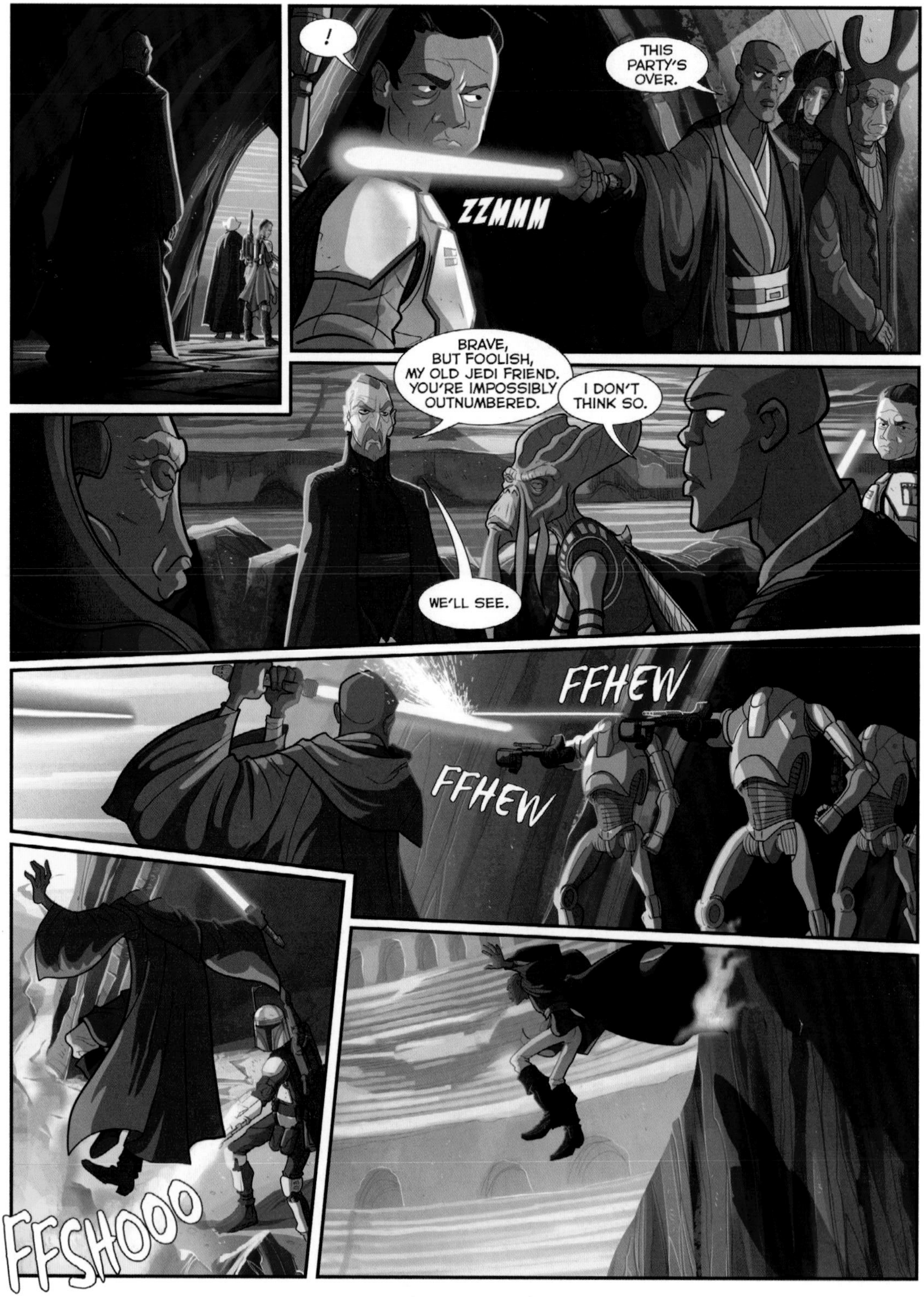
!
THIS PARTY'S OVER.
ZZMMM
BRAVE, BUT FOOLISH, MY OLD JEDI FRIEND. YOU'RE IMPOSSIBLY OUTNUMBERED.
I DON'T THINK SO.
WE'LL SEE.
FFHEW
FFHEW
FFSHOOO

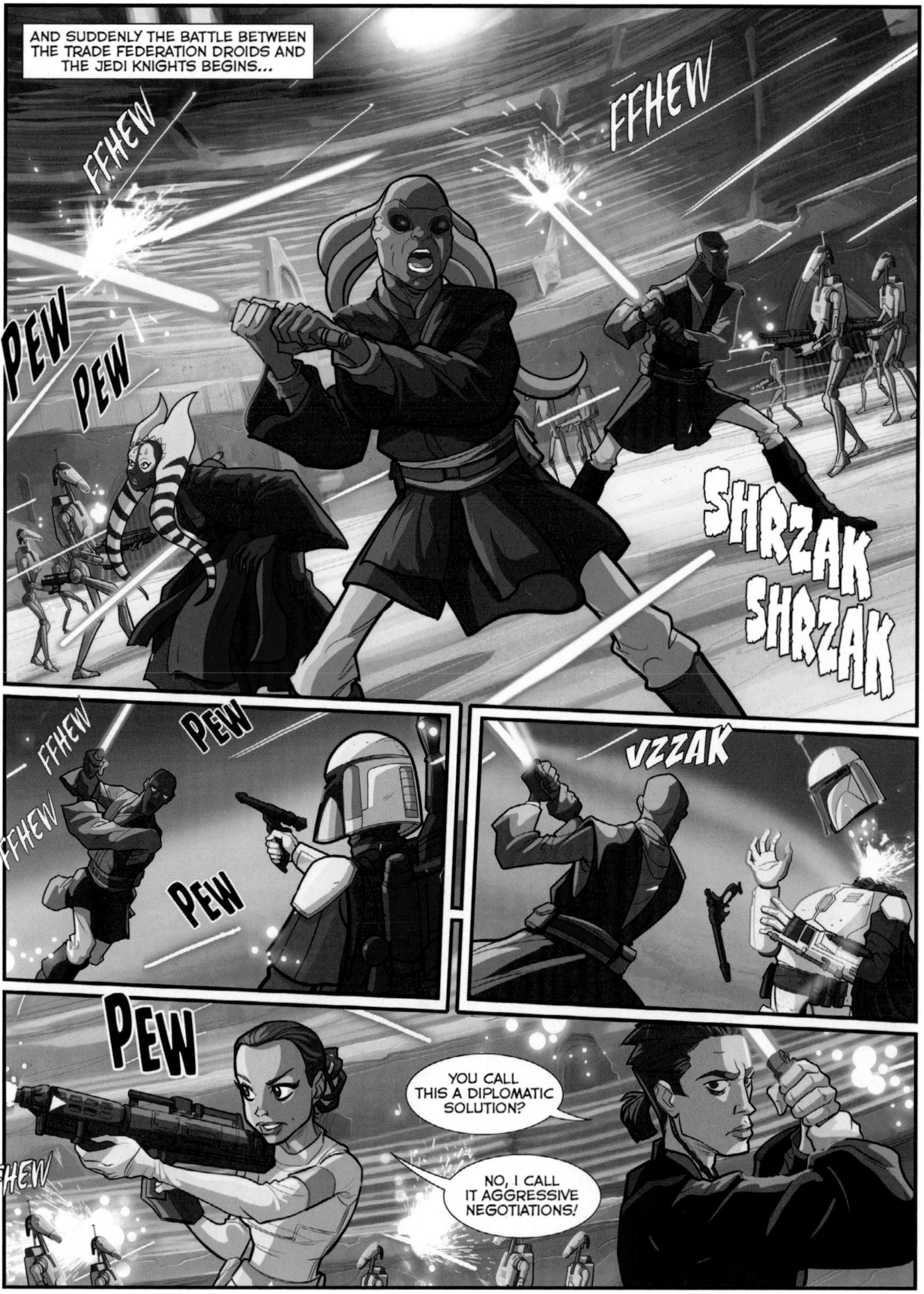
AND SUDDENLY THE BATTLE BETWEEN THE TRADE FEDERATION DROIDS AND THE JEDI KNIGHTS BEGINS...
FFHEW
FFHEW
PEW
PEW
SHRZAK
SHRZAK
FFHEW
PEW
FFHEW
PEW
VZZAK
PEW
YOU CALL THIS A DIPLOMATIC SOLUTION?
FFHEW
NO, I CALL IT AGGRESSIVE NEGOTIATIONS!

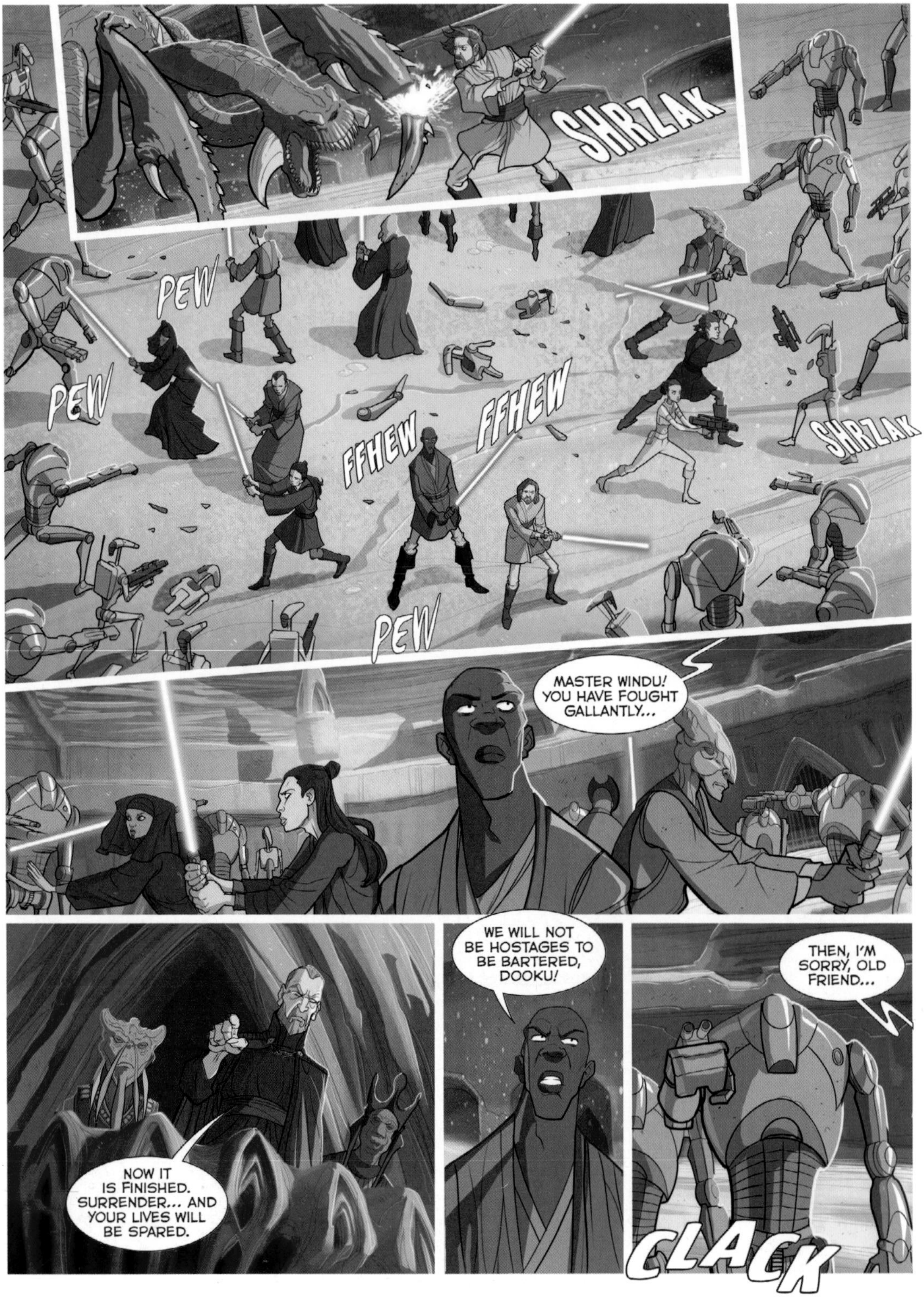
SHRZAK
PEW
PEW
FFHEW
FFHEW
SHRZAK
PEW
MASTER WINDU! YOU HAVE FOUGHT GALLANTLY...
NOW IT IS FINISHED. SURRENDER... AND YOUR LIVES WILL BE SPARED.
WE WILL NOT BE HOSTAGES TO BE BARTERED, DOOKU!
THEN, I'M SORRY, OLD FRIEND...
CLACK

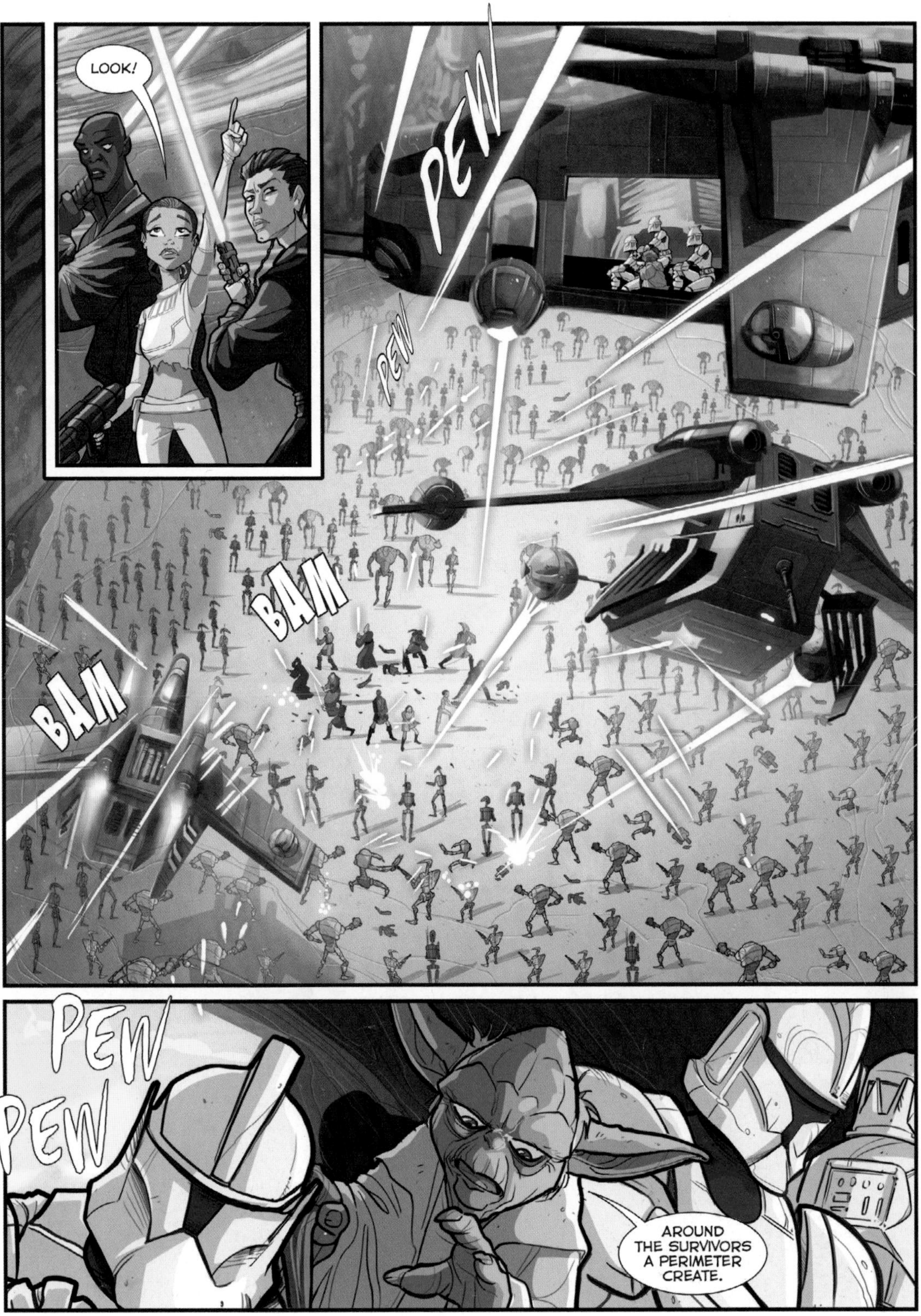
LOOK!
PEW
PEW
BAM
BAM
PEW
PEW
AROUND THE SURVIVORS A PERIMETER CREATE.

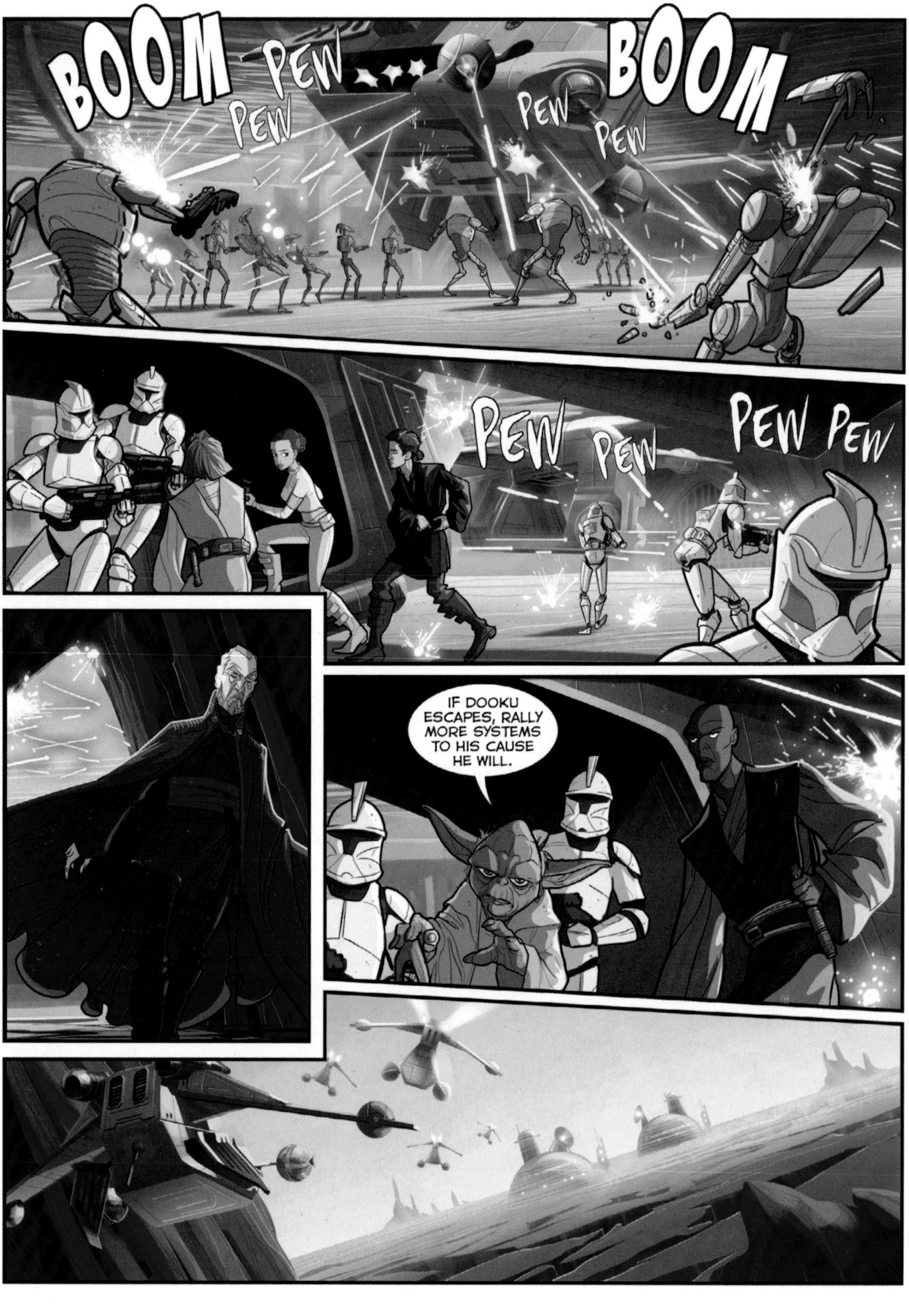
BOOM
PEW
PEW
BOOM
PEW
PEW
PEW
PEW
PEW PEW
IF DOOKU ESCAPES, RALLY MORE SYSTEMS TO HIS CAUSE HE WILL.

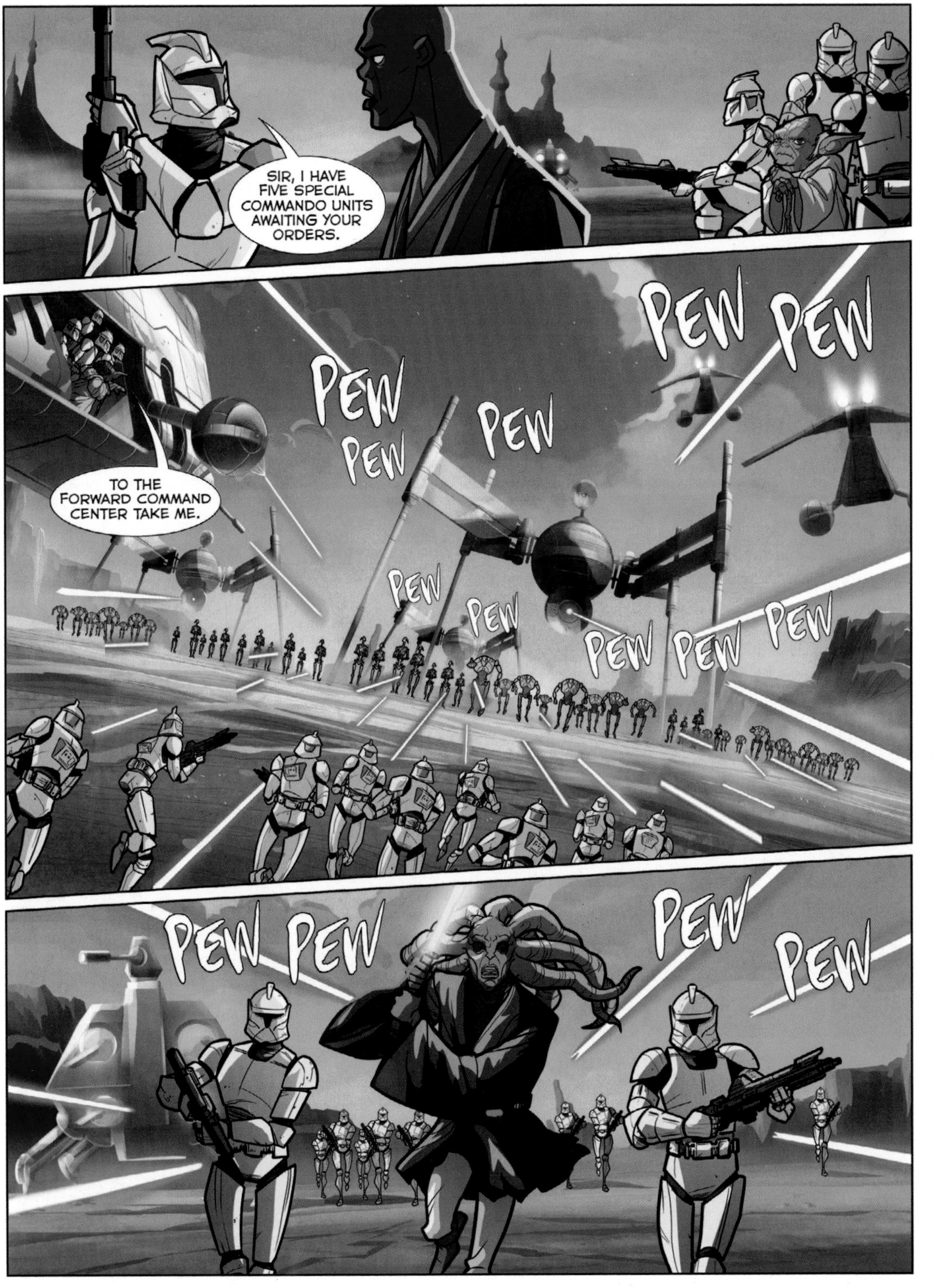
SIR, I HAVE FIVE SPECIAL COMMANDO UNITS AWAITING YOUR ORDERS.
PEW
PEW
PEW
PEW PEW
TO THE FORWARD COMMAND CENTER TAKE ME.
PEW
PEW
PEW PEW PEW
PEW PEW
PEW
PEW

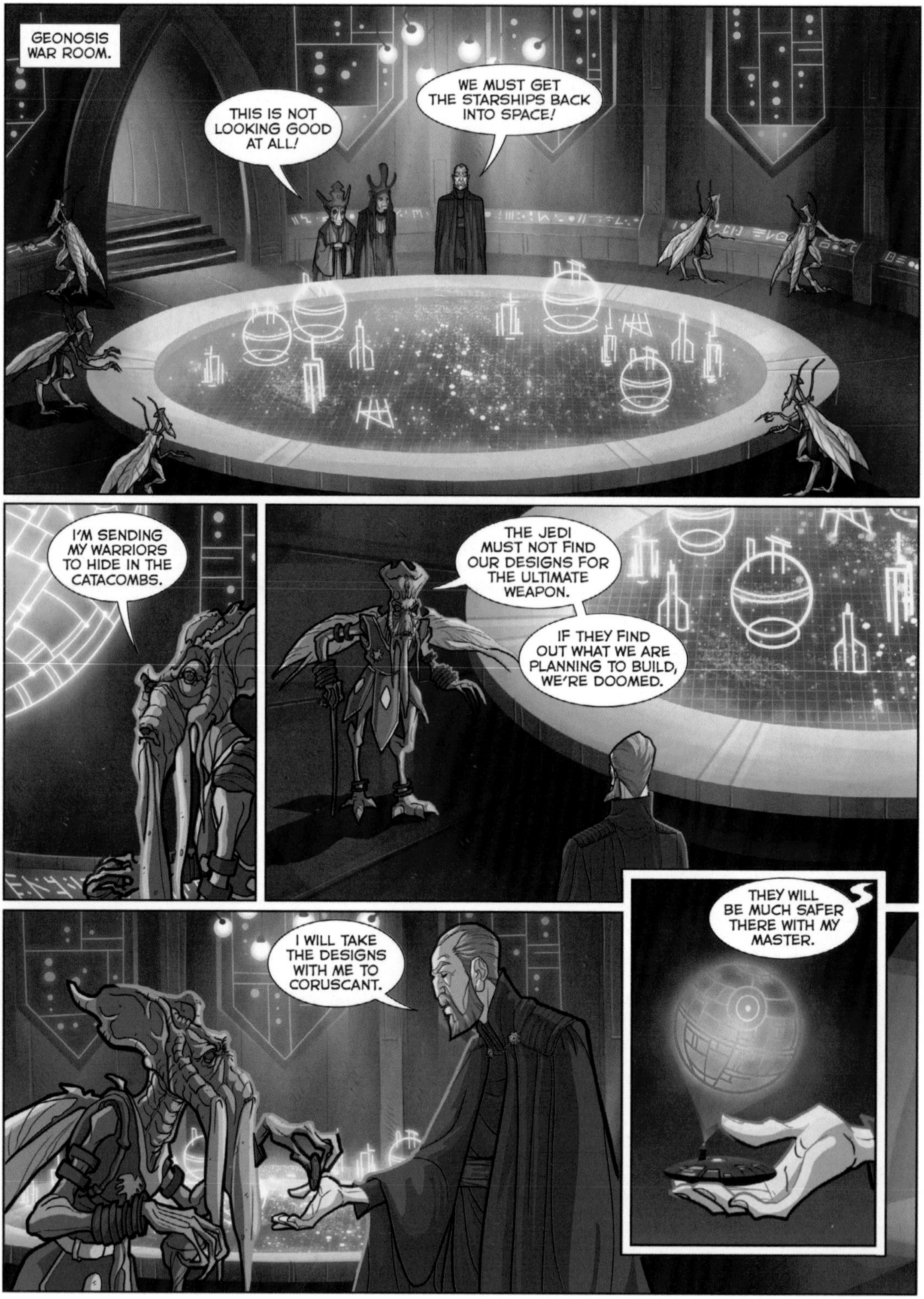
GEONOSIS WAR ROOM.
THIS IS NOT LOOKING GOOD AT ALL!
WE MUST GET THE STARSHIPS BACK INTO SPACE!
I'M SENDING MY WARRIORS TO HIDE IN THE CATACOMBS.
THE JEDI MUST NOT FIND OUR DESIGNS FOR THE ULTIMATE WEAPON.
IF THEY FIND OUT WHAT WE ARE PLANNING TO BUILD, WE'RE DOOMED.
I WILL TAKE THE DESIGNS WITH ME TO CORUSCANT.
THEY WILL BE MUCH SAFER THERE WITH MY MASTER.

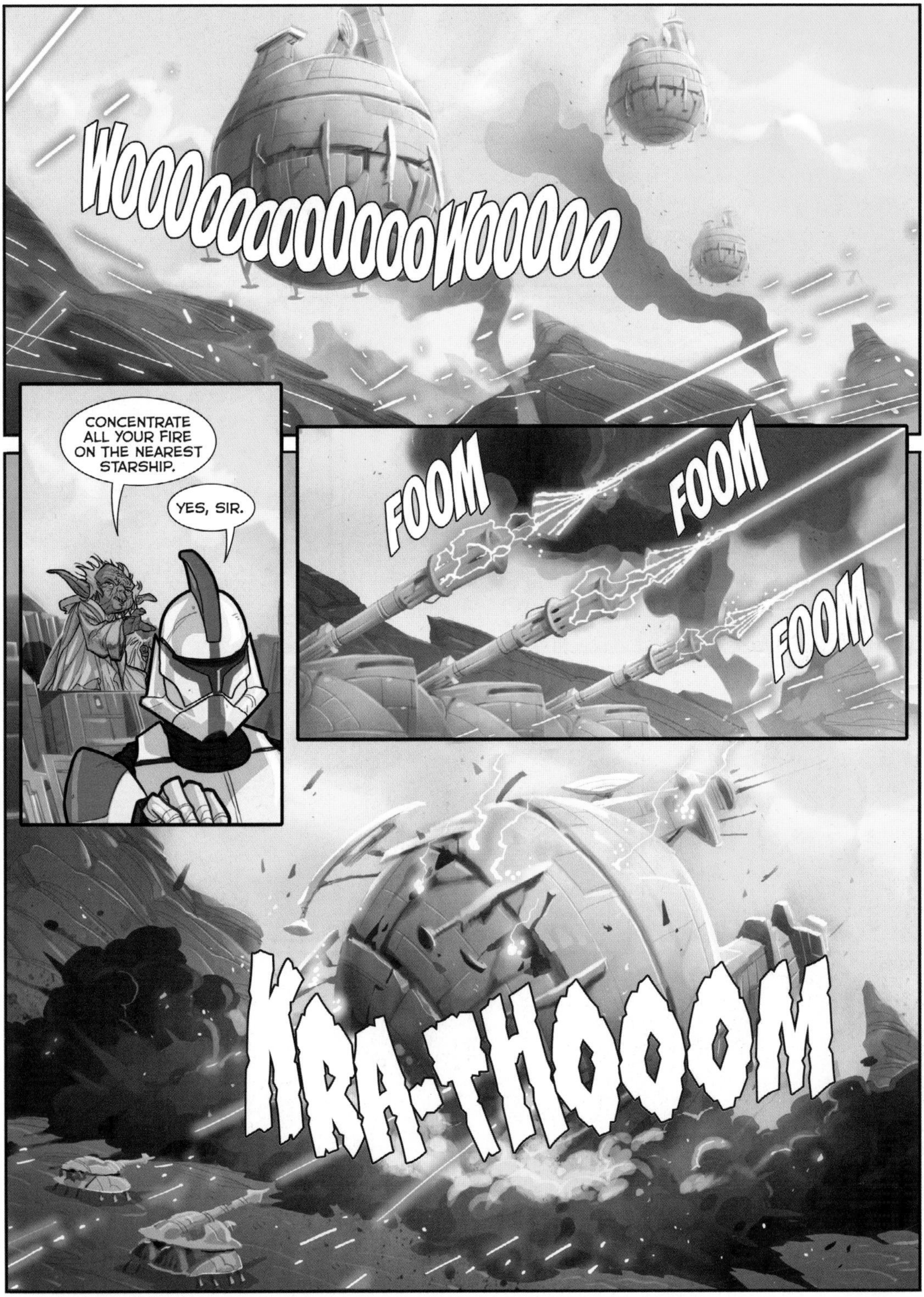
WOOOOOOOOOOOOOWOOOOO
CONCENTRATE ALL YOUR FIRE ON THE NEAREST STARSHIP.
YES, SIR.
FOOM
FOOM
FOOM
KRA-THOOOM

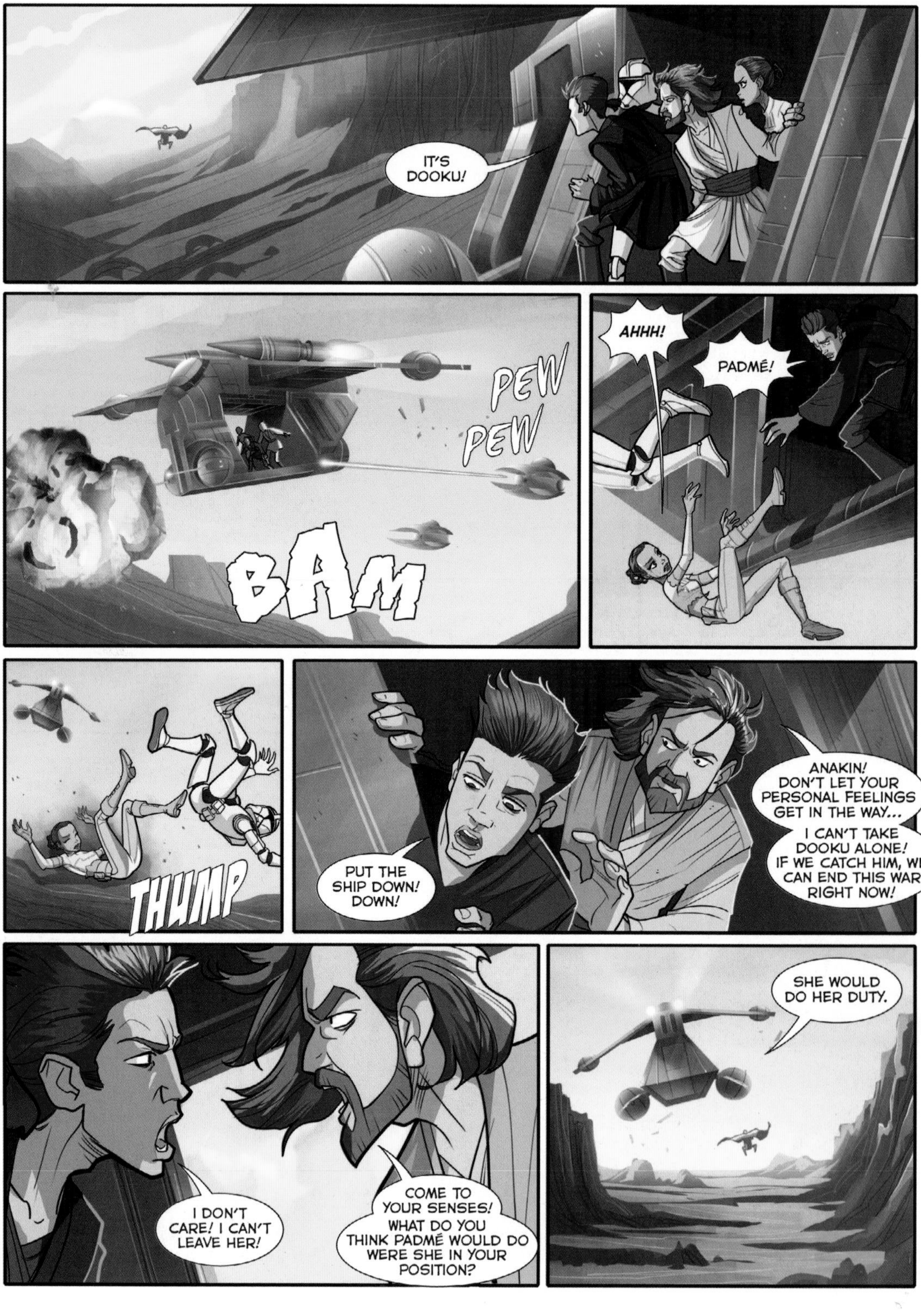
IT'S DOOKU!
PEW PEW
BAM
AHHH!
PADMÉ!
THUMP
PUT THE SHIP DOWN! DOWN!
ANAKIN! DON'T LET YOUR PERSONAL FEELINGS GET IN THE WAY...
I CAN'T TAKE DOOKU ALONE! IF WE CATCH HIM, WE CAN END THIS WAR RIGHT NOW!
I DON'T CARE! I CAN'T LEAVE HER!
COME TO YOUR SENSES!
WHAT DO YOU THINK PADMÉ WOULD DO WERE SHE IN YOUR POSITION?
SHE WOULD DO HER DUTY.

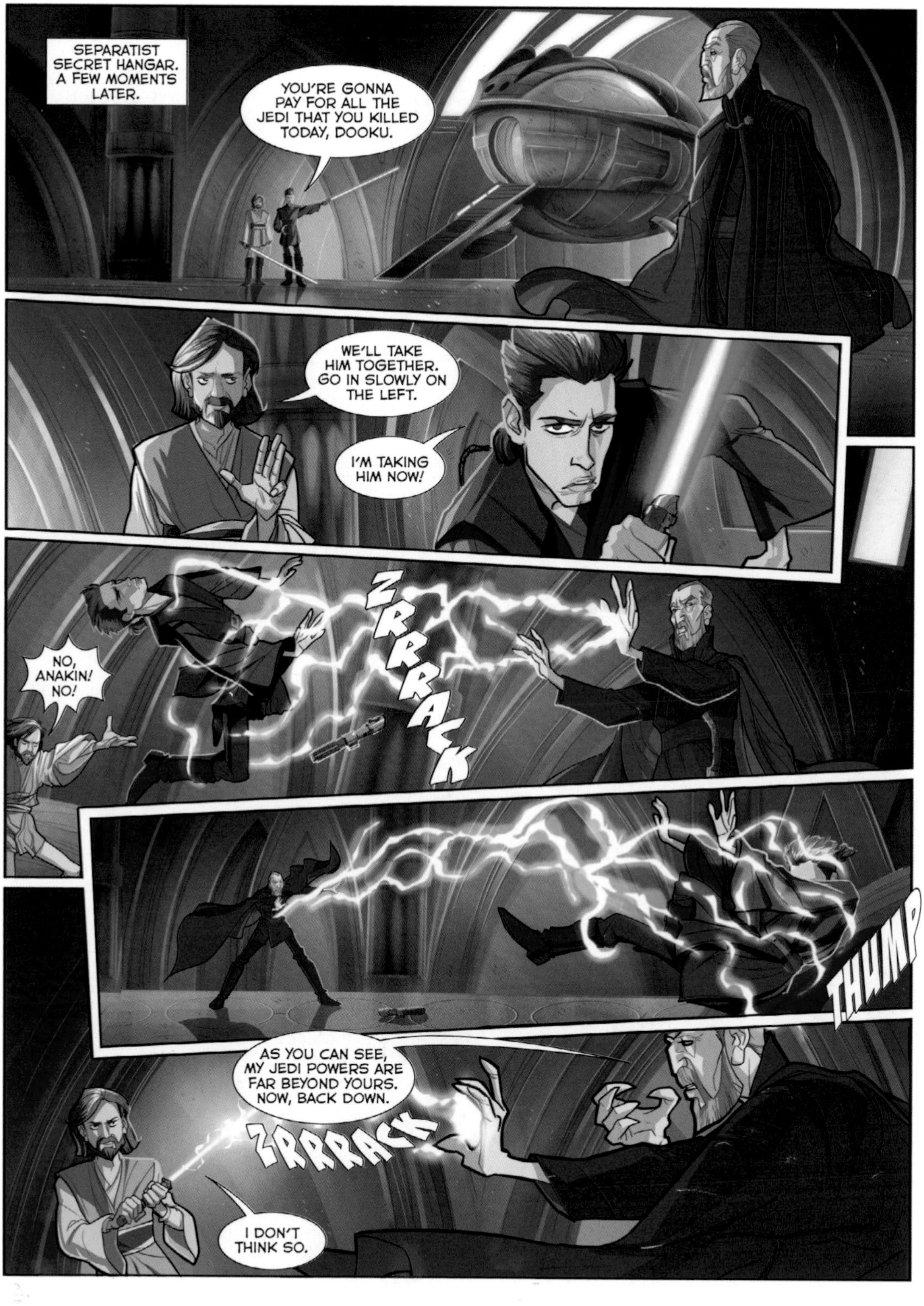

SEPARATIST SECRET HANGAR. A FEW MOMENTS LATER.
YOU'RE GONNA PAY FOR ALL THE JEDI THAT YOU KILLED TODAY, DOOKU.
WE'LL TAKE HIM TOGETHER. GO IN SLOWLY ON THE LEFT.
I'M TAKING HIM NOW!
ZRRRACK
NO, ANAKIN! NO!
THUMP
AS YOU CAN SEE, MY JEDI POWERS ARE FAR BEYOND YOURS. NOW, BACK DOWN.
ZRRRACK
I DON'T THINK SO.

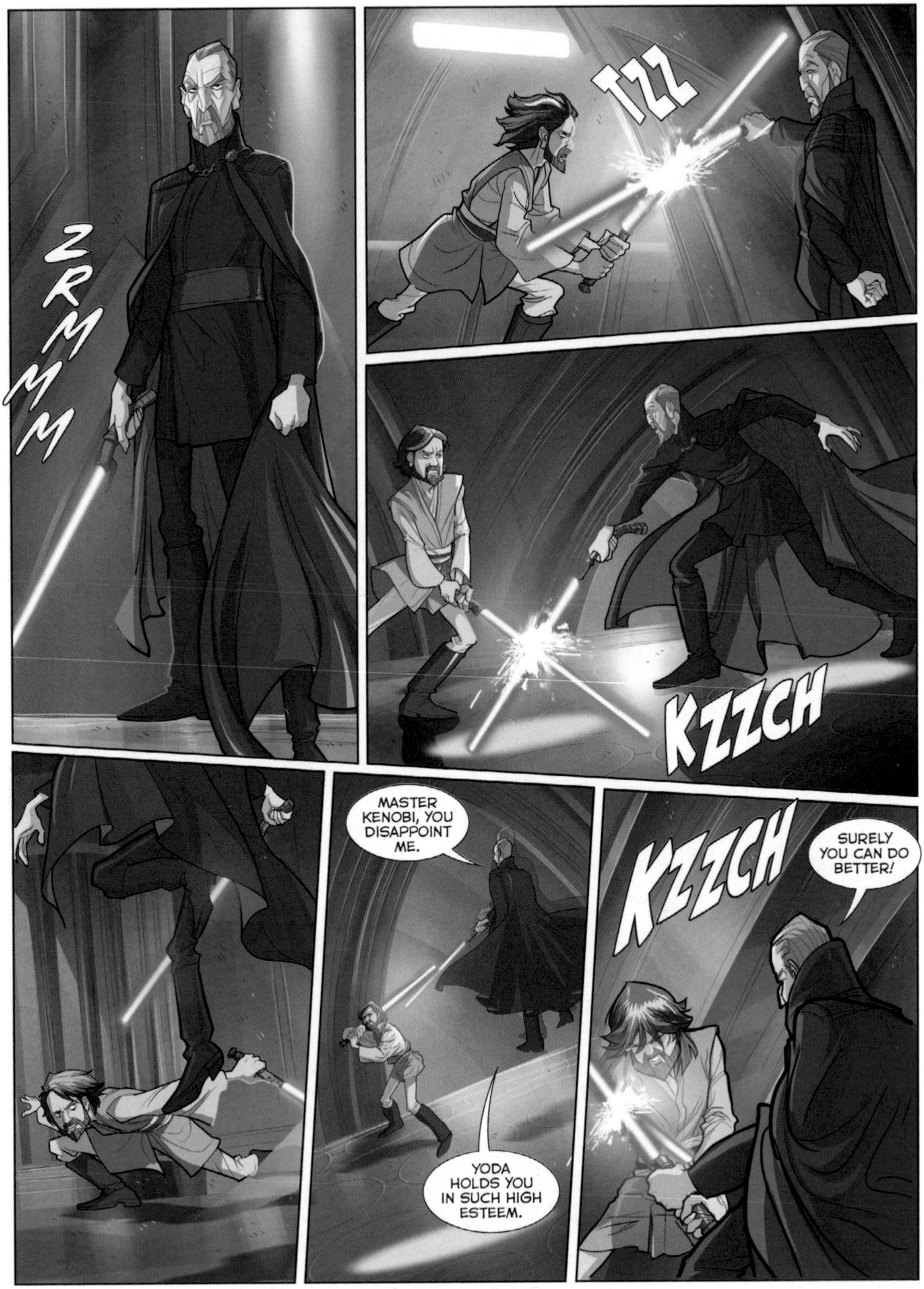
ZRMMMM
TZZ
KZZCH
MASTER KENOBI, YOU DISAPPOINT ME.
YODA HOLDS YOU IN SUCH HIGH ESTEEM.
KZZCH
SURELY YOU CAN DO BETTER!

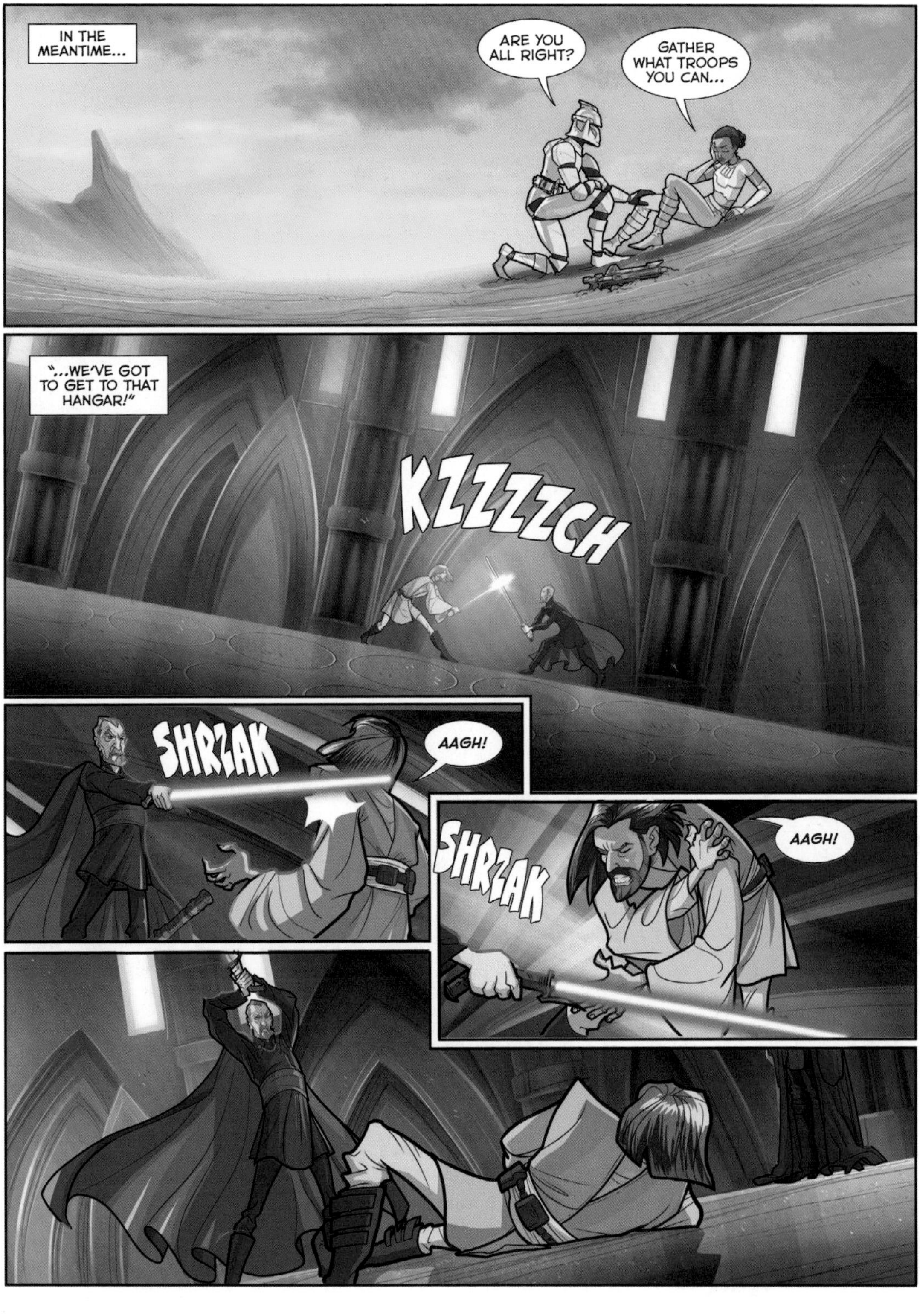
IN THE MEANTIME...
ARE YOU ALL RIGHT?
GATHER WHAT TROOPS YOU CAN...
"...WE'VE GOT TO GET TO THAT HANGAR!"
KZZZZCH
SHRZAK
AAGH!
SHRZAK
AAGH!

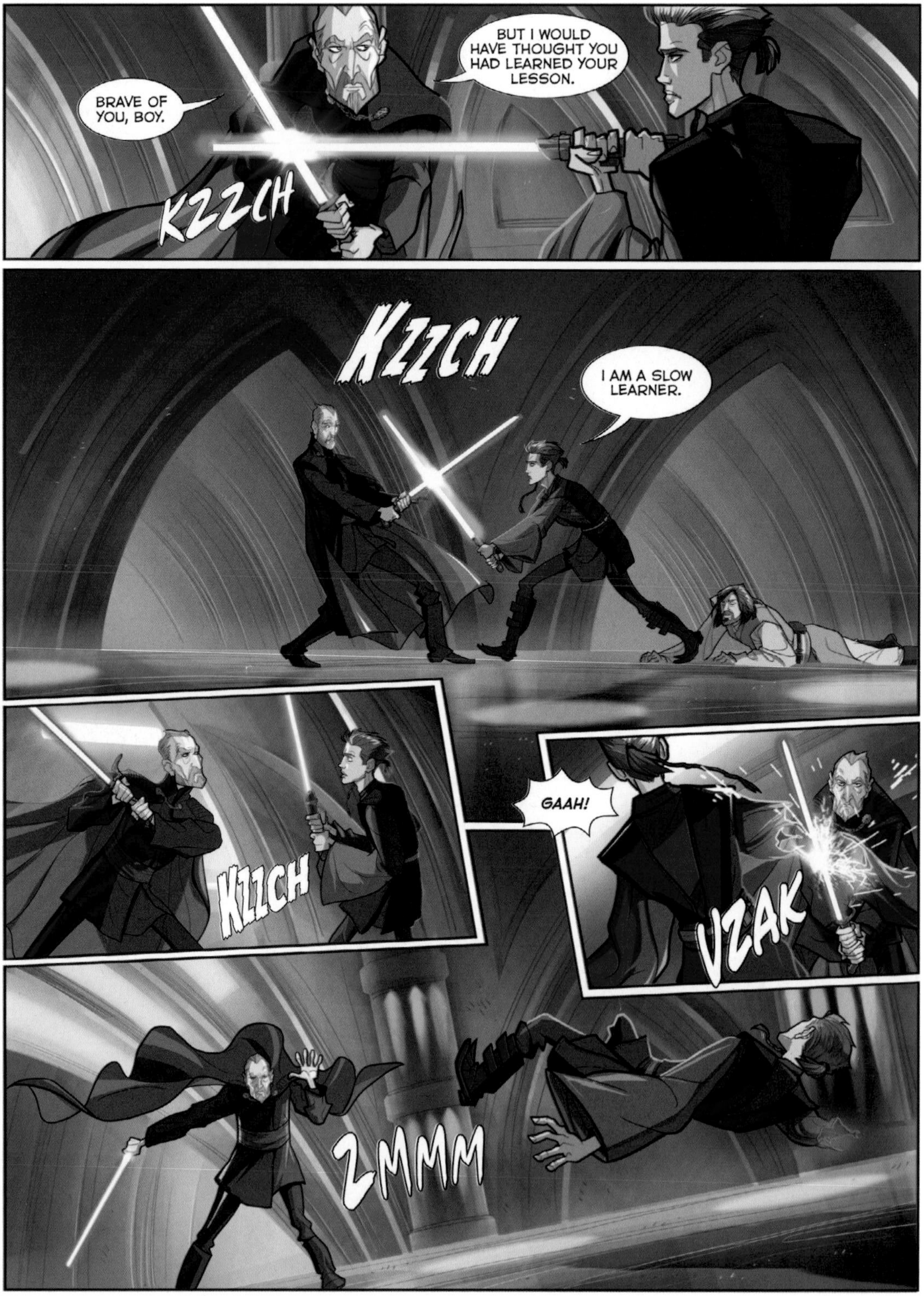
BRAVE OF YOU, BOY.
BUT I WOULD HAVE THOUGHT YOU HAD LEARNED YOUR LESSON.
KZZCH
KZZCH
I AM A SLOW LEARNER.
KZZCH
GAAH!
VZAK
ZMMM

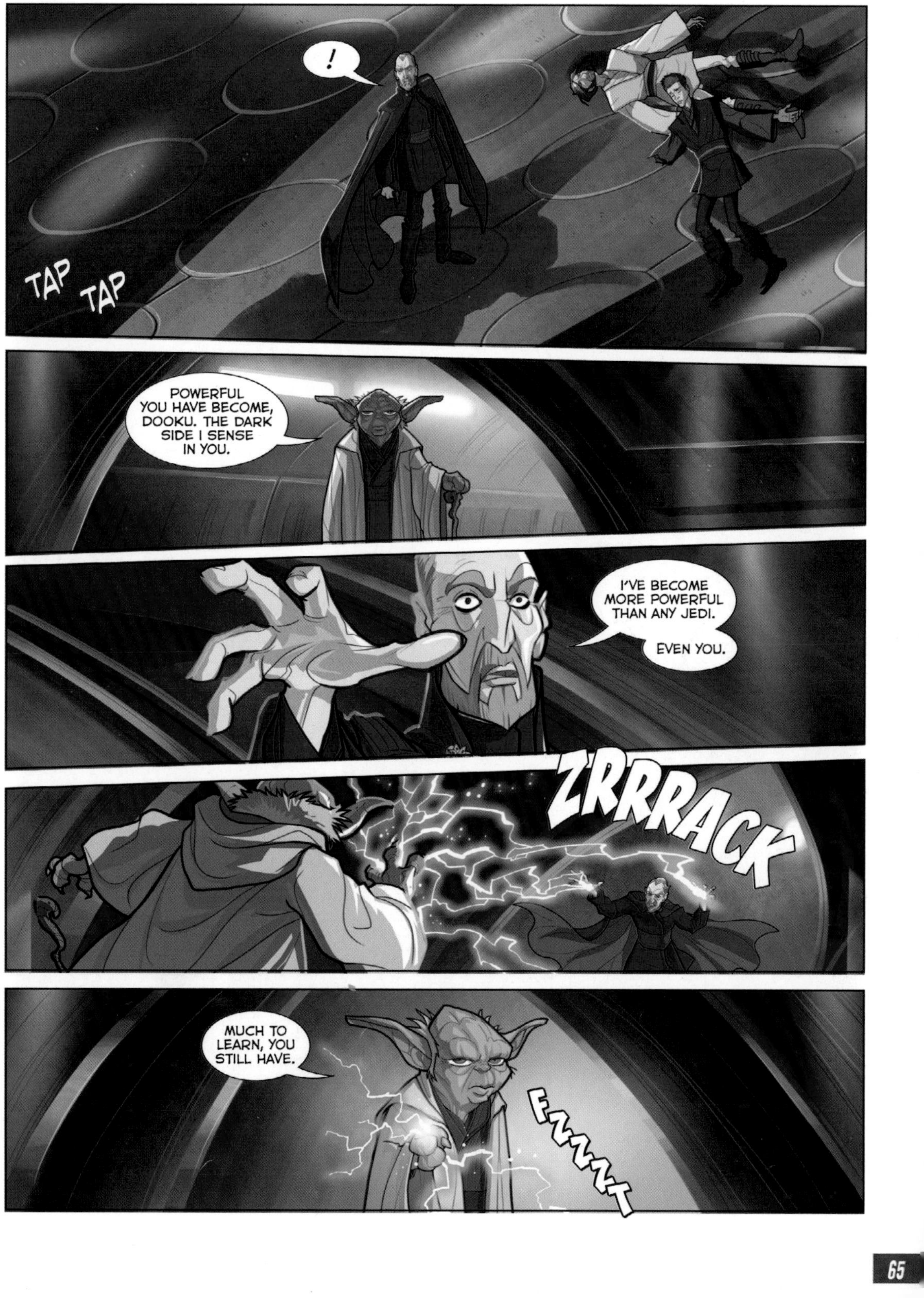

!
TAP TAP
POWERFUL YOU HAVE BECOME, DOOKU. THE DARK SIDE I SENSE IN YOU.
I'VE BECOME MORE POWERFUL THAN ANY JEDI.
EVEN YOU.
ZRRRACK
MUCH TO LEARN, YOU STILL HAVE.
FZZZZT

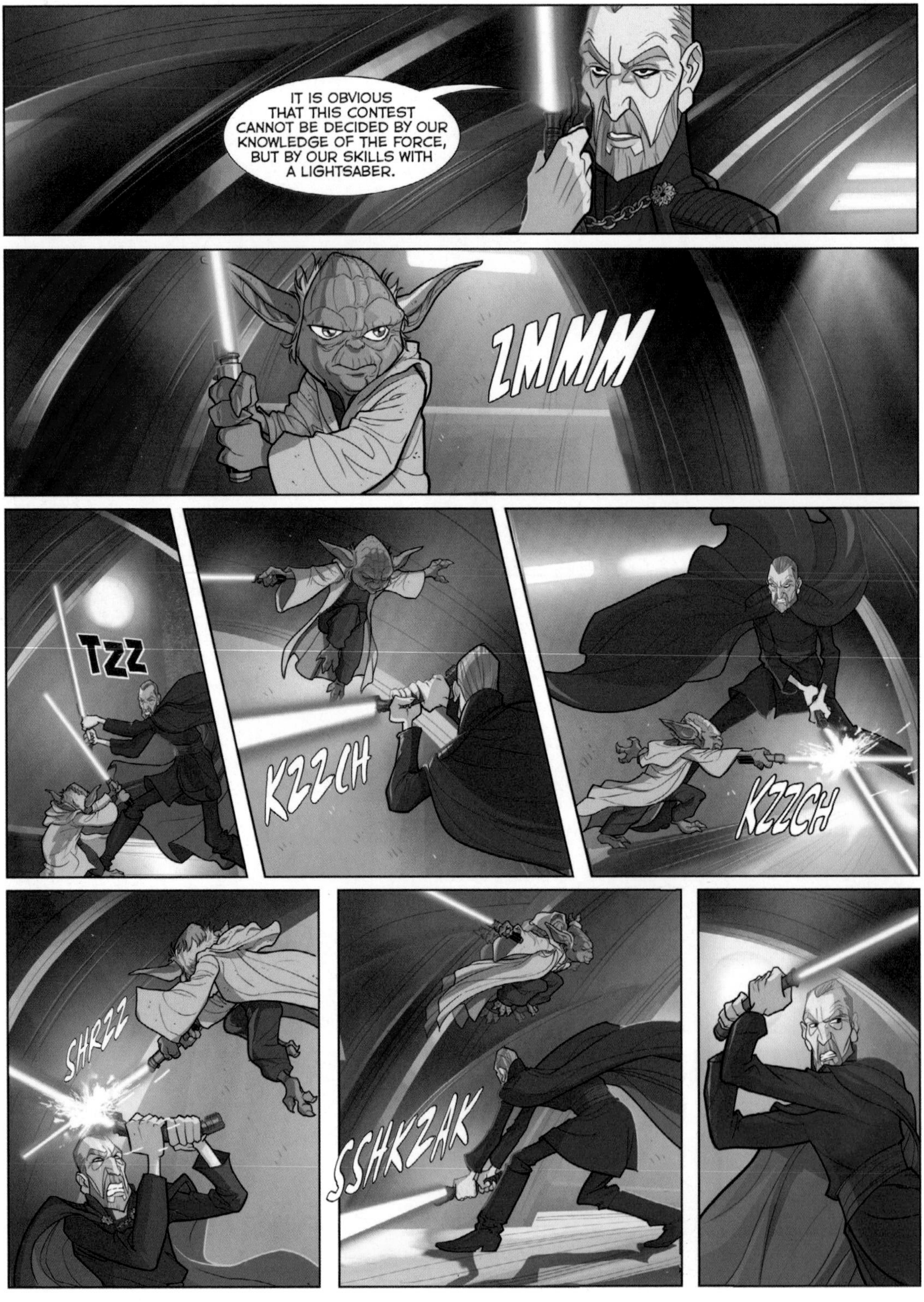

IT IS OBVIOUS THAT THIS CONTEST CANNOT BE DECIDED BY OUR KNOWLEDGE OF THE FORCE, BUT BY OUR SKILLS WITH A LIGHTSABER.
ZMMM
TZZ
KZZCH
KZZCH
SHRZZ
SSHKZAK

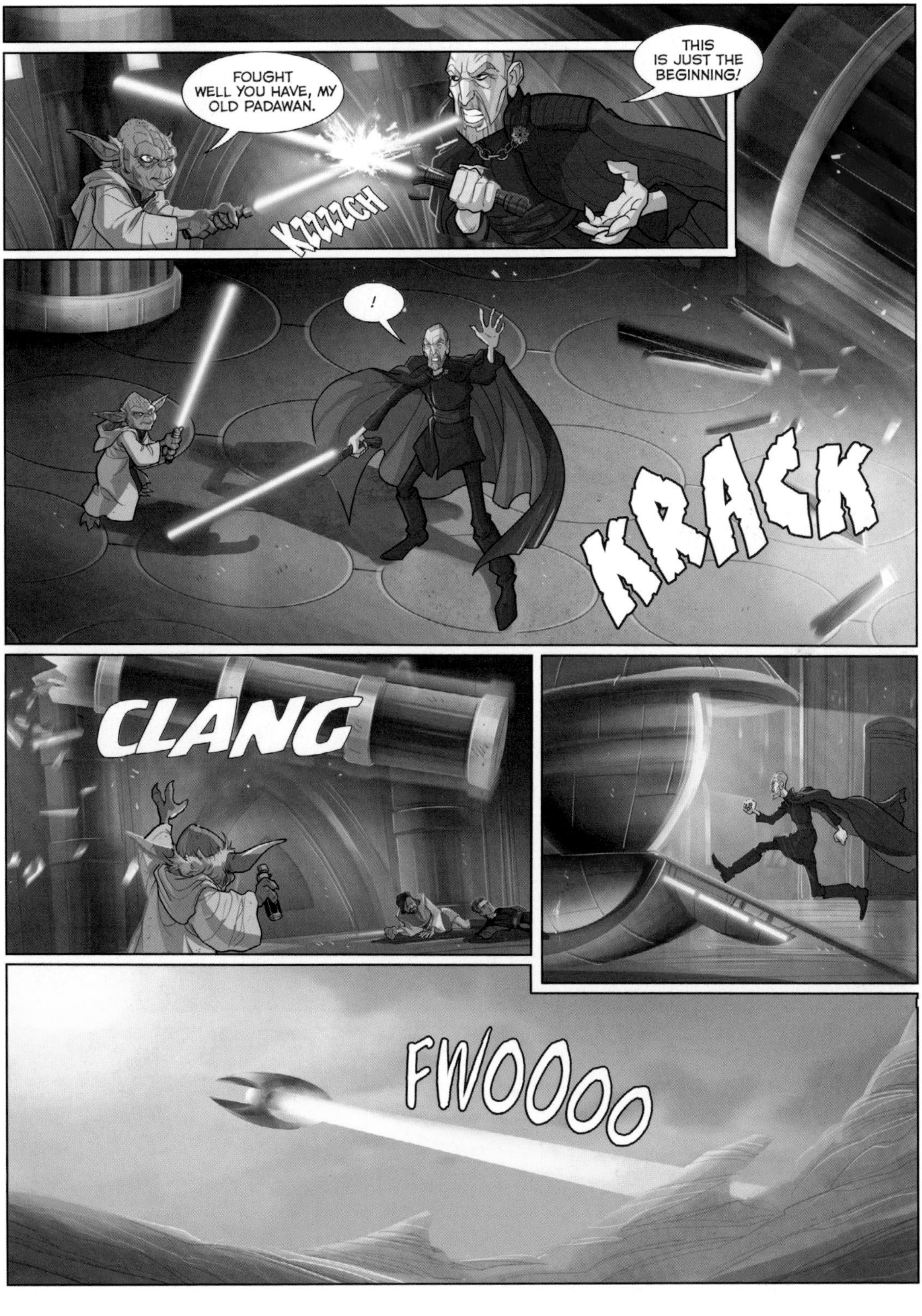
FOUGHT WELL YOU HAVE, MY OLD PADAWAN.
THIS IS JUST THE BEGINNING!
KZZZZCH
!
KRACK
CLANG
FWOOOO

THOOM

ANI!

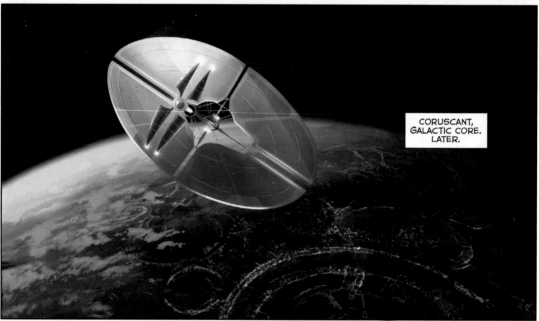

CORUSCANT, GALACTIC CORE. LATER.

THE FORCE IS WITH US, MASTER SIDIOUS.

WELCOME HOME, LORD TYRANUS. YOU HAVE DONE WELL.

I HAVE GOOD NEWS FOR YOU, MY LORD. THE WAR HAS BEGUN.

EXCELLENT. EVERYTHING IS GOING AS PLANNED.

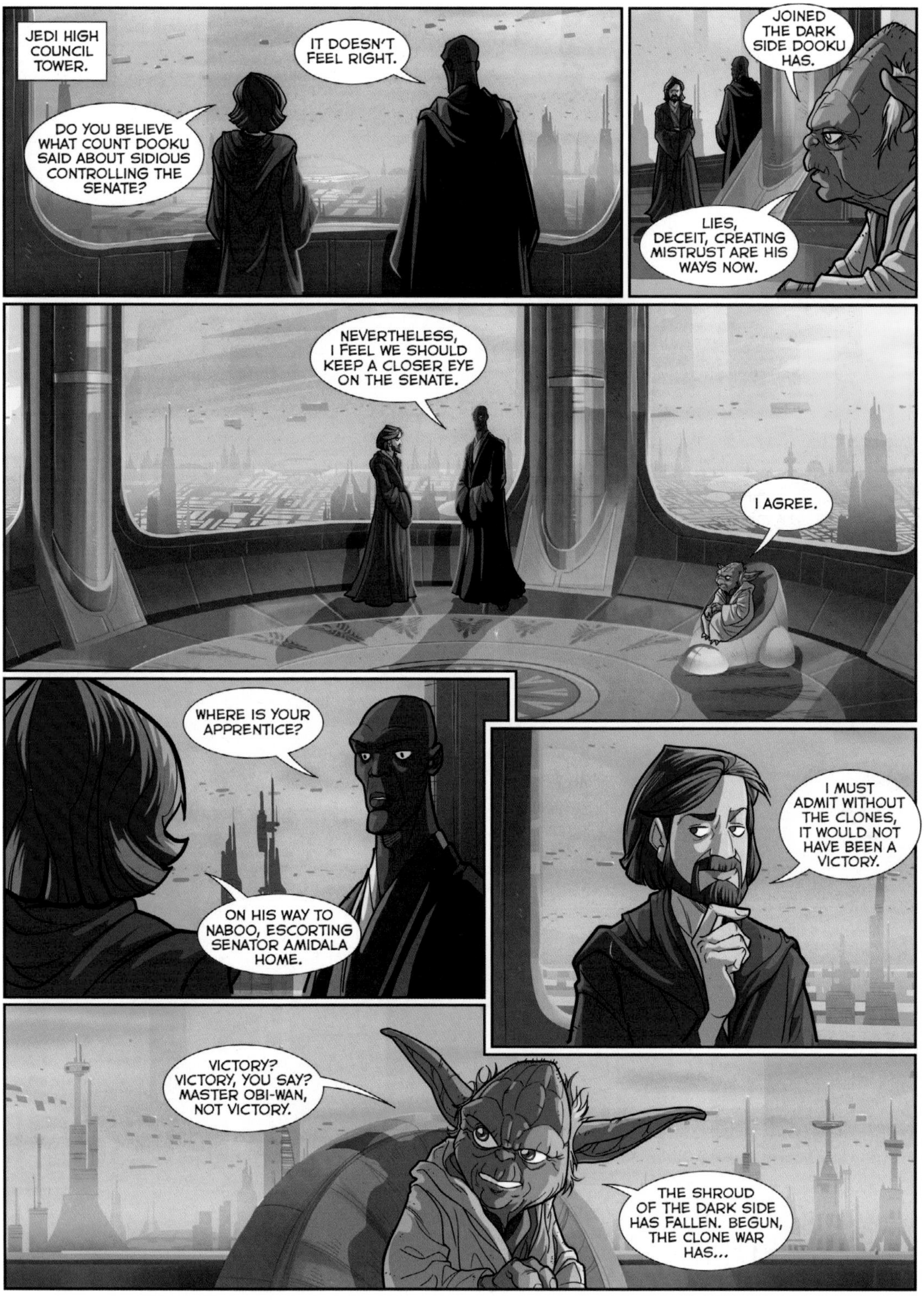
JEDI HIGH COUNCIL TOWER.
IT DOESN'T FEEL RIGHT.
DO YOU BELIEVE WHAT COUNT DOOKU SAID ABOUT SIDIOUS CONTROLLING THE SENATE?
JOINED THE DARK SIDE DOOKU HAS.
LIES, DECEIT, CREATING MISTRUST ARE HIS WAYS NOW.
NEVERTHELESS, I FEEL WE SHOULD KEEP A CLOSER EYE ON THE SENATE.
I AGREE.
WHERE IS YOUR APPRENTICE?
ON HIS WAY TO NABOO, ESCORTING SENATOR AMIDALA HOME.
I MUST ADMIT WITHOUT THE CLONES, IT WOULD NOT HAVE BEEN A VICTORY.
VICTORY? VICTORY, YOU SAY? MASTER OBI-WAN, NOT VICTORY.
THE SHROUD OF THE DARK SIDE HAS FALLEN. BEGUN, THE CLONE WAR HAS...

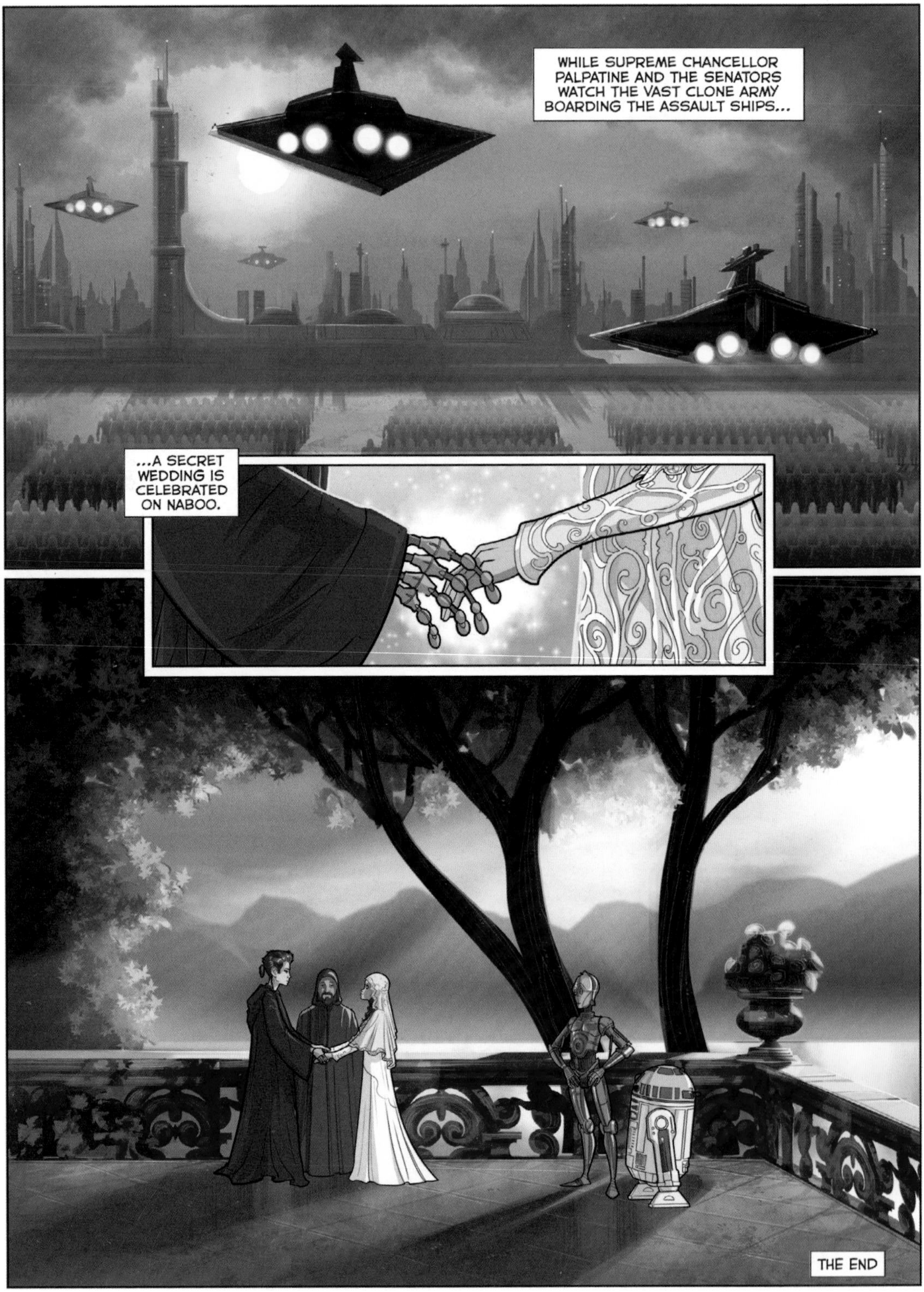
WHILE SUPREME CHANCELLOR PALPATINE AND THE SENATORS WATCH THE VAST CLONE ARMY BOARDING THE ASSAULT SHIPS...
...A SECRET WEDDING IS CELEBRATED ON NABOO.
THE END

"THE DARK SIDE CLOUDS EVERYTHING. IMPOSSIBLE TO SEE THE FUTURE IS..."

Yoda

CREDITS

Manuscript Adaptation
Alessandro Ferrari
Character Studies
Igor Chimisso
Layout
Ingo Römling
Clean Up and Ink
Andrea Greppi, Igor Chimisso, Marco Dominici,
Monica Catalano
Paint (background and settings)
Davide Turotti
Paint (characters)
Kawaii Creative Studio
Cover
Crissy Cheung
Special Thanks to
Michael Siglain, Jennifer Heddle,
Rayne Roberts, Pablo Hidalgo,
Leland Chee, Matt Martin

DISNEY PUBLISHING WORLDWIDE
Global Magazines, Comics and Partworks

Editorial Director
Bianca Coletti
Editorial Team
Guido Frazzini (Director, Comics)
Stefano Ambrosio (Executive Editor, New IP)
Carlotta Quattrocolo (Executive Editor, Franchise)
Camilla Vedove (Senior Manager, Editorial Development)
Behnoosh Khalili (Senior Editor)
Julie Dorris (Senior Editor)

Design
Enrico Soave (Senior Designer)

Art
Ken Shue (VP, Global Art)
Roberto Santillo (Creative Director)
Marco Ghiglione (Creative Manager)
Stefano Attardi (Illustration Manager)
Portfolio Management
Olivia Ciancarelli (Director)
Business & Marketing
Mariantonietta Galla (Marketing Manager),
Virpi Korhonen (Editorial Manager),
Kristen Ginter (Publishing Coordinator)
Editing – Graphic Design
Absink, Edizioni BD
Contributors
Carlo Resca

For IDW:
Editors:
Alonzo Simon and Zac Boone

Collection Design:
Nathan Widick

Lucasfilm Credits:
Robert Simpson, Senior Editor
Michael Siglain, Creative Director
Phil Szostak, Lucasfilm Art Department
Matt Martin, Pablo Hidalgo, and Emily Shkoukani,
Story Group

Based on the story by George Lucas

For international rights, contact licensing@idwpublishing.com

ISBN: 978-1-68405-856-3

25 24 23 22   1 2 3 4

Nachie Marsham, Publisher • **Blake Kobashigawa**, VP of Sales • **Tara McCrillis**, VP Publishing Operations • **John Barber**, Editor-in-Chief • **Mark Doyle**, Editorial Director, Originals • **Lauren LePera**, Managing Editor • **Joe Hughes**, Director, Talent Relations • **Anna Morrow**, Sr. Marketing Director • **Keith Davidsen**, Director, Marketing & PR • **Topher Alford**, Sr. Digital Marketing Manager • **Shauna Monteforte**, Sr. Director of Manufacturing Operations • **Jamie Miller**, Sr. Operations Manager • **Nathan Widick**, Sr. Art Director, Head of Design • **Neil Uyetake**, Sr. Art Director, Design & Production • **Shawn Lee**, Art Director, Design & Production • **Jack Rivera**, Art Director, Marketing
Ted Adams and Robbie Robbins, IDW Founders

www.IDWPUBLISHING.com

Facebook: facebook.com/idwpublishing • Twitter: @idwpublishing
YouTube: youtube.com/idwpublishing • Instagram: @idwpublishing